"Jamie"

A one man's struggle with Good and Evil

by

Dorothy LaRock Skinner

First published by AuthorHouse 05/27/04

ISBN: 1-4184-6285-3 (e-book)
ISBN: 1-4184-2346-7 (Paperback)

This book is printed on acid free paper.

I DEDICATE THIS BOOK TO THE FOLLOWING PEOPLE
TO
SANDY WHO WAS MY INSPIRATION
TEDDY< MY GRANDSON WHO WAS MY COMPUTER WIZ
JEREMY WHO HAS BEEN MY ENCOURAGER
BECKI WHO HAS BEEN MY PROVIDER
JAMIE WHO BEARS THE NAME GRACEFULLY
BETSY WHO IS MY SECRET KEEPER
AND MY LOVING HUSBAND LUTHER WHO
HAS BEEN MY HOUSEKEEPER WHILE WORKING ON THIS
BOOK!

"JAMIE'S FAMILY MAKES A VISIT"
Chapter 1

Jamie paced back and forth across the worn out wooden floor. The way he kept pacing, one might think that he was trying to wear the old mission floor thinner then it already was! But that was the furthest from his mind. The thing that he had on his mind at this time was the telegram! The one that had just been brought to him by the messenger boy, Renjo. Anyway Jamie was beside him self in thought. For you see, along with the telegram, and the fact that he was soon to be visited by his brother Frankie, and that with Frankie's family, came many memories rushing through Jamie's mind. These was memories that he hadn't took the time to remember in such a long time. There were things that he wasn't so sure about! Things that he had thought about so many times, but still kept them in some far off corner of his mind. Some things that he had kept so closed in his mind, that he faintly was aware of them; he just wouldn't let them surface in his thoughts, so that he could face them square on.

It truly was a long time ago! Twelve long years to be exact, that had passed since he seen his brother, or anyone else in his family. Then he thought of his brother's wife Lorraine. How would he feel toward her? How would he act being around her? Better yet, even if he managed to keep his cool, how will she react toward him? He had done a good job convincing himself up until now, that he was over her. But now as he thought about her, he wondered just how did they really feel about each other? After twelve long years apart, he wondered just what it would feel like to see her again, especially since she was now Frankie's wife!

"But Jamie!" He said to himself, as he so often talked as though there was two of him. "Will that old feeling come back again?" As he thought about this, he moaned in a self- agonized plea; "Oh my God! Please! Please let that feeling that I had for her be gone!"

That was the thing that was really bothering him at this particular moment. He walked over to the window, and stared out it. He stared a long, long time. He let his thoughts and feelings go back into his past. Back to Lorraine. He felt that exciting warm feelings that he had had for her. He remembered the day that they had met, the day that he first laid his eyes on her. That day he laid his claim on her in his mind. That was the day he vowed in his heart that she would be his forever! She was so beautiful, and she caught his eye right off with her auburn red hair, and those soft green, with a tint of blue eyes, and her small five foot frame. The very minute he saw her made him want her so bad! At the thought of her brought back a sensuous, but sad feelings. He shook his mind free of the thought of her, and returned back to the present, as he uttered aloud.

"I just felt we could be great for each other. If only I had been different, then we could have had a better chance together!" Turning away from the window, he threw his hands up in despair, as he remembered just how he was back then.

"I know what I put her through!" I just can't blame God for not letting me keep her. All that pain, and sorrow, why was I like that to her? She deserved something better! That is for sure! Even after she fell in love with Frankie, I could not leave her alone! I was just so jealous of them two! I just wanted to do something that would separate them. I didn't care what, just as long as I could come between them! If I really had loved her all that much, then why, I ask myself now, didn't I try to make her happy?"

All those ugly things that he had done came rushing like a violent storm raging back at he now. He remembered the time that he tried to take both of their lives while driving his car off the road over a steep embankment. He recalled that time clearly, the jealous feelings that he had when he thought of her ever being with anyone else, let lone his younger brother Frankie. He recalled stepping on the gas pedal until it wouldn't go any more and letting go of the steering wheel, letting the car plunge over the embankment. He remembers the sounds of Lorraine's screams, then the smashing of glass, the tumbling, the rolling, and rolling over and over, and then the silence. That horrible silence! There it all was before him once again, and even though it was just a memory now, it all seemed so real, and he covered his face with his hands as the thought came to him so real! He wanted to block it all out again once more.

"Oh my God, thank You so very much that you was looking out for us two that day, even though I didn't deserve Your protection back in those awful days!"

Coming back from that bad night mare of Jamie's past, he realized that it was getting later, and he really had to hurry and get going! Oh, but those memories! They just would not let him rest! Once again, as though he had no control over them he picked up the telegram again. His eyes went over the lines, searching through it as though it there was some thing important that he had missed.

"They are bringing Timmy." He said; as his mind went back to a little blonde haired boy. A little boy who had his Father's blue eyes. He was just five when Jamie left him behind.

"Will Timmy remember me?" He asked himself. In his heart he hoped that he would, but he also wondered and worried just what he would think of his dad now.

"Timmy, I wouldn't blame you one bit if you hated me for not only what I have done to you, but not being there for you! Not being a dad to you." All these thoughts and many, many more raced through his mind. Timmy's life was sure one of a misfit. Jamie was not a good father to Timmy and he was never there for him from day one!

"Oh how much I owe to you now Timmy boy!" He said out loud. "How I wish that I could change things. How I wish I had been a better father to you...at the most, I should have been there for you when you were growing up! I have failed so many people, especially those who I should have been there for."

Then, almost like an electrical shock, Jamie's mind turns to his daughter Dana. He was ashamed to think it but, he had not seen her since she was just a small baby. Twelve years ago, he left her behind. Oh what a terrible, horrible time that was for him! He never allowed himself to know Dana. She seemed to him to be more like a part of a bad, bad dream! Not because of anything that she had done, but what was going on in his life at that time. Then in his mind, another tragic scene…the sad tragic moments he had shared with Dana's mother Merle.

"Merle baby, I did love you, and I love you yet! I miss you still!" He fairly cried in agony. Then for the first time in twelve years he let himself remember Dana's mother Merle.

"Oh it hurt so badly then!" He cried out again. "Merle baby, now I know things, things that you tried so hard to tell me back then. Now I know many things! It is so clear to me now. God has opened my eyes, and helped me to see all those things that you Merle baby wanted me to know! God has given me a new life now with Nadine, because you Merle baby wanted to go be with Jesus! You loved Him so much! You wanted me to love Him too, but at that time I could not see what you saw! How very dumb I was at that time! How very lost I was too, back then!" He paused for a long time, as though he was thinking things through, then as though it would make a difference now, he blurted out;

"Well I do know now! I do see plainly now Merle baby, I really do! Someday you will know, someday Merle baby you will see that He is my Saviour, my all!"

Jamie glances up at his clock, and seeing how the time has gone so fast, it brings him back to the present. It was getting much too late! Time was not waiting for him to do all this thinking! Turning away from all his thoughts a few minutes, he made a mad attempt to pick up things, to tidy up the place a little. He wanted the house to be as inviting and neat as possible for his company that night. He wished that Nadine had not had to have left for the church meeting so early, but he knew about how things went at the little church on meeting nights.

"Besides!" He said to himself again; "If she had of waited for me, I would not have been able to do all this thinking!" He sort of laughed to himself. "And besides she does a really splendid job with the song services."

He was sure that he would be way late. If only he could stop his thinking, his remembering! His thoughts turned to the children again. His children. He silently prayed that Frankie had did a good job at bringing them up well. But why should he doubt that? Frankie always had a good way in rearing kids. He thought about Frankie, and as he thought about his brother, he thought of how well bred, and immaculate Frankie was, he knew that surely Frankie would bring his children up in the same way. He recalled just how strict Frankie had been to his own child; surely that was his brother's way. Trying to dismiss all these thoughts from his mind, he went and dressed fast, for it was way past the time that he should have left!

"I just know that the church is going to be packed, it usually is! They will be looking for their preacher, and he won't be there! Even Nadine will be wondering where I am, and will be sending someone out to find me!" He thought to himself. He felt a nervous type of excitement as he took a quick look around the room and then grabbed up his Bible, and notes, and headed out the door, letting it bang behind him. All kinds of thoughts ran through his mind as he walked down the road to the church. So many doubts and fears entered his mind, as he wondered just how he could handle the forth coming situations that loomed within just hours away.

"I must not let this thing over take me." He mumbled to himself. "I already have a good life here with Nadine, and the children, and the church, and I must not let anything spoil or come between Nadine and me! That is the reason why I cannot let Nadine know about my old loves, and my life before her. I must devise a plan that will buy me time to be able to deal with this situation I have.

"Oh my God, what would You have me to do? I have no plan! But I know that You do, so please reveal Your plane to me! Please help me in this stressful time of my life!"

He walked the rest of the way to the church with his head bowed in prayer, and pleadings.

"STARTING TO UNDO JAMIE'S SECRET"
CHAPTER 2

The little church was packed as usual. It seemed as though every one had a smile on their faces, and every body was singing full blast! The songs came out to meet Jamie's ears, as he approached the steps of the church. Jamie felt relieved, and a sense of joy filled his heart. This was his new life, and he was happy to be a part of it. He, as he so often did, wondered just how he deserved to be so happy. He hoped that his not so well thought of plan of how to deal with what was coming up, would not change his new life. When he thought of the One that made him feel so happy, and at peace, he then felt the joy of serving his Master. He knew in his heart that he had become a new man when he started to let Jesus take over his life. Jesus had done so much for him, he just had to be happy about it!

Nadine felt a sense of relief too, as she heard her husband's deep voice blend in the last stanza of the song that they were singing. She wondered just what had taken him so long, but she knew that all was well now that he had arrived, and took the pulpit He smiled at her, as he opened his Bible, and greeted the people.

"Today I am asking that God, the most glorious Father of our Lord Jesus Christ to give to you all, the wisdom to see clearly and really understand just who Christ is, and all that He has done for you and me. I pray that your hearts will be flooded with this light, so you can see something of the future that He has called you to share. I want you to realize that God has been made rich because we who are Christ's have been given back to Him through His wonderful Son Jesus. I pray," Jamie's sermon went on, and his congregation listened intently to their Pastor. They too have gained since Jamie has been with them. They loved to hear Jamie tell them just how much Jesus loved them! Much of Jamie's sermons came directly from the Gospel. He had his notes, but always ended up speaking as the Holy Spirit moved him to. Often times he allowed silence, and meditations, so to give the Holy Spirit room to move upon each repentant soul. He allowed time to let the Love of Christ penetrate the hearts of the people. There was many who came to Christ this way.

Jamie loved his people, as much as they loved him. Often times he would hold up his sermon just to comfort a troubled member. When this happen not only Jamie, but the people would rally around giving that one soul any comfort they too could offer. Jamie knew just how important it was to feel so bad and lost, and then fined out that there is hope! That somebody does care! He remembered when the devil control over him, and his life had, and what a miserable man he had been! At that time he had just lost his wife Merle, and he felt that he had sinned way beyond any hope, or help. He was sure that nobody cared. He had sunk very low. However, Somebody did care enough to stoop down, and pick him up. Somebody who really did care! At that time in his life, he felt that he had destroyed everything that he had ever loved. But Jesus cared. Jesus was there for him. Now Jamie must care, and be there for these people too. Because Jesus had time to listen to him, he too, while walking in Jesus' footsteps, in turn takes the time too. It was obvious to Jamie that this was part of the cause that Jesus had lifted him up and thaught him that there was some worth in Jamie. The things that had been so important, and dear to Merle, were some of the things Jamie had to learn. The things that were so necessary for Jamie's salvation, those were the things that he had to pass on to those other needed souls.

"I pray that you will begin to understand just how incredibly great His power is to help those of us who believe in Him. We must never forget that once we were like heathens, and that we were called Godless, and unclean. But God has put all things under His feet, and made Jesus the Supreme head of the church, which is, you and me. We make up His body, which is filled with Himself the Author and Giver of everything, everywhere. Because of God's kindness we human souls can be saved by trusting Christ our Saviour…!" Jamie said as he started to conclude his sermon. "And even trusting is not of our selves, it is a gift from God. Salvation is not a reward for the good that we have done, so none of us can take credit for it. It is God Himself who has made us what we are and given us new lives from Christ Jesus. It was our lives, which He planned out for us long ages ago. We are to help ourselves, by helping others. With God, all things are possible! Though your sins be as scarlet, Jesus said; I will make them white as snow. I will put them far from you, I will blot them out, just as though they never where."

While the closing song was being sung, Jamie thought about his sermon. These thoughts had brought back a scene to his mind. It was far away in another church. It was far bigger, and lovelier then this church. It was a big white church with a stately steeple at the top. He saw himself kneeling at the alter, and he was being forgiven. The Comforter had come to him. He felt, for the first time, his burdens being lifted, and the joy that comes into a sinner's heart when the Holy Spirit comes in and take possession, and also brings in forgiveness. There had been years of sanctification for him, but he felt justified right then through the precious blood of Jesus, and His grace. Jesus had become so close to him, so very close! Since then everything depended upon Jesus, and what He would have Jamie do. All these thoughts and feelings brought Jamie to this place in his life. The song ended, and they all bowed their heads for prayer.

After the usual procedure of greeting friends, and shaking their hands, it was time to depart for their mission home. Walking up the road toward home, Jamie broke the news about the telegram that he had received earlier to Nadine. He told her about Frankie being his brother, but he did not fill her in as to who else would be coming with Frankie other then it was just all of Frankie's family. He asked her to do him a big favor, and also trust him for what he was about to ask her to do. She agreed, not knowing what he was about to say. He asked that she would not let on to these people that he and she were married, until it seemed right. That was the way he put it! He said he would

9

let her know when it was the right time to tell about it. He also asked that she stay with one of her friend's place until he could work out somethings that had to be worked out. Nadine felt anxious, and sort of fearful for what her husband had asked her to do, but she agreed, because of the way he had asked her, and partly because she feared in her heart to meet these strange people of Jamie's, too. Jamie told her about his daughter Dana, and how he had not ever been there for her, and he told Nadine that he wanted Dana to get to know him before he asked her to accept a stepmother. Jamie didn't really feel in his heart that this was the right, or honest approach, but he feared silently about how things would go not only between him and Dana, but between the rest of the family too. Besides understanding the type of life that Dana was use to, for living with his brother Frankie, she was sure to be use to a rich enviroment. Frankie was really rich, and very well off. Much, much richer then anything Jamie now has to offer her. So he figured that it would take a lot of extra convincing and lots of special love, and attention, and even understanding on Jamie's part, to even have Dana accept the life style that Jamie had to offer her. He knew this, because he was once very well off, and he remembers how had felt about the less fortunate! There was even a good chance that Dana just might be prejudice toward Nadine, and her Native American background! Jamie did not know just how Dana would be! He did not want to let on to Nadine, until he was sure. So that was one reason why he did not encourage Nadine in any way, except that she stay with her friend, and not let on that there was any involvement between them at all. This arrangement would only be for a short time, so Nadine agreed. She could come to the house as a housekeeper, or as a friend, because Jamie would probably need her assistance in the house, but she was to remain silent about their relationship until further notice from her husband.

She was not to let on, or show any signs that they where married, or had any kind of close relationship with Jamie, other then just being friends. Nadine really did not like this arrangement, but said nothing. Jamie felt reluctant about making this arrangement, but they did not have much time to work it out any other way. He wanted so badly to get his daughter back!

Therefore, they walked in silence for some time. He was feeling that this was being dishonest to both Nadine, and Dana, but he loved them both, and did not want to lose either of them. Other wise, doing it any other way, he just might lose them both! He also did not want to do anything that God would disapprove of. But yet he felt that this was the only answer in such a short notice!

He felt a sense of relief too to be able to face this alone without Nadine. He hoped in his heart that he had no feelings that he hadn't delt with about his past, but deep down he felt very unsure, and was relieved to know that he could possibly deal with them, and never hurt Nadine because of it.

Actually, he did not really know just how he did feel, especially about Lorraine. More so then how he felt Dana would fit in. Nadine on the other hand, also felt relieved about the arrangements, mainly because she really did not want to know how Jamie had lived before her. She also was afraid of her feelings. Both was feeling fear, and doubt, and both was afraid to bring it up to each other, or even mentioning it for fear that the other one might not understand. They silently tried to think of something to say to each other to take the presure off. Therefore, they remained silent for sometime. When the silence seemed almost unbearable, Nadine spoke up.

"It will be alright my darling>"She said, trying to reassure him. "It will work out okay. You love me still, huh?" She replied, trying to reassure herself too.

"Yes, I love you." He said back;

"Then I love you too! Please do not worry will you? We will be praying that it will all work out for the good! However, do remember, I love you very much! I am willing to wait for you forever if it takes that long! It it means your happiness! Just do not worry about me, I will be okay. You won't be that far away that I couldn't come to you if I needed to." She said as she smiled up at him. But down in her heart, she didn't feel that sure that all was going to be all that right, and perfect. It seemed to her that he agreed too readily with this agreement. She wondered just what he was hiding from her and these thoughts tugged at her subconscious mind, Then Jamie replied;

"Okay, I guess that is how we will do it, but I sure hope that this is the right way to go." In addition, all the rest of the way home, they walked in silence, both deep in their own thoughts.

11

Dorothy LaRock Skinner

"IT'S BEEN SO LONG"
CHAPTER 3

A few hours after they returned home, there was a big white Lincoln pulled in their driveway. Jamie knew at a glance

That it was his brother's car.

"They are here." He announced in a rather calm voice. He tried to hold back the excitement that he felt, as he thought about seeing any of his family again. Alternatively, any of those who he had left behind from his home back in Kentucky.

Nadine smiled at him, for she could see that her husband's excitement was mounting. He was oh so anxious to see them again, but acted somewhat reluctant about letting it show.

"Go for it sweetheart!" She told him.

Without any more hesitations, he went out side and walked toward the car. The dark haired man that got out of the car, Jamie recognized as his brother Frankie. Time had passed, but it seemed to have been good to his brother, for he had not changed at all! Lorraine came around the car as the two brothers where hugging and patting each other on the backs, exchanging their greetings. Jamie rather stiffens as he glanced over at Lorraine. He thought that she looked radiantly happy and most beautiful as he had ever remembered. Flash backs of her paraded through his mind. They reminded him of how much he had cared for her back then. His heart pounded within him, as though at some great point it would burst into a million pieces! He slowly walked toward

13

her, and gave her a hug. He hoped in his heart that he did not hold her too close for her to recognize just how good and right it felt to him, to hold her in any way. With every effort, he tried to make it just a casual embrace. He thought how good it was to see them both again. It had been so long since he had seen any of them. He realized that because he never took the time for 'good bys' there was never any closure for any of them, when he left those behind in Kentucky.

"It's been so long!" He blurted out. "Much too long, I will say!" He gazed at Lorraine again, and thought to himself that she was as beautiful as ever, but he still wondered just what his true feelings about her yet. He wondered just what he felt. It sure felt good to be that close to her, and smell her perfume again. On thinking about how she made him feel, left him with some worried reservations in his mind concerning her. He silently prayed that he could be strong about her. His thoughts were still on her as he saw the children getting out of the car, and coming toward him. Feeling more relieved, he calmed his inner thoughts, and feelings, as he started to focus on the children.

"This is Timmy." Frankie felt that he had to introduce each of them to him. Jamie turned to Timmy. With tears mingled with nervous laughter, they hugged. Timmy was not that little boy that his father remembered. He had already grown beyond his age in size. He is seventeen now, and very masculine. He was quite handsome, and showed many traits of belonging to Jamie. Jamie could tell that he had been reared elegantly by the way he was dressed, and his displayed dignity. Pride swelled up in Jamie's heart when he saw his son.

Next in line was Dana. The long awaited years for both of them finally brought father and daughter to this very precious moment! Jamie has felt a wave of weakness come over him as he looked at his daughter for the first time! She looked so much like her mother that it made Jamie's throat tighten up. It was as though he was looking at Merle! His mind came back to reality, when Frankie took a hold of Dana's hand, and brought her forth to meet her father.

"This is your daughter Dana! Isn't she just as pretty as can be? Frankie said; sort of nervously, waiting for Jamie's responds.

"So this is my Dana!" Jamie muttered, searching for words that seemed to have lost their way out. What does one say in a situation like this? He thought. He stretched out his hand toward her. Still wondering just what to say, for he felt strangly quilty as he looked into her eyes. He knew that she was his very own flesh and blood, and he loved her very much, He felt very sad too, because he left her behind, and never showed her love that he should of. Now he did not really know her at all! He was not sure of what, or how much she knew about him. It surely felt somewhat strange to him.

"So this is my Dana?" He repeated, as though he still could not believe it. "How very pretty you are!" He exclaimed. He wanted to hug her too, as he had Timmy. He wanted to say, I am your father, and that everything is going to be all right now, because I will never leave you again. I am sorry for leaving you behind! I love you more then words can say! He wanted to say all this, and reassure her, but he knew he should not just yet. This just was not the right time and place. He knew that it would be a long time, but it would happen someday, if ever, before he could tell her all this, it will happen he was sure! It would take a lot of loving, and a lot of kindness and understanding, and much, much more patience before it could happen. Then finally while with all this hashing things out in his mind, it automatically came out past the big lump in his throat, and he said;

"I am your father, Dana but perhaps you already know that." There was a silence, a long unconfortable silence, with Dana just staring at him, and not moving. Her gray-blue eyes reminded him so much of Merle's. He thought of how she so resembled her mother. After what seemed like a lifetime, with no one saying a word, she finally turned to Frankie as though he could tell her what to say. As though she did not want to choose her words by her self.

"It is okay, Danny, this is your real father of whom you have heard so much about. The one that you have longed to meet. This is your father that we have always told you about." Frankie assured her.

Dana then turned back to Jamie. She reluctantly put her arms around his neck, and hugged him. Jamie felt the reluctance, but realized that he did not deserve even a hug! He had turned his back on her when she was a newborn. He recalled the day when he laid her down into her crib, and turned his back on her and just walked right out of her little life! He did not even look back! He hardly recalled what she even looked like. All those years he had hardly took the time to even think about her. He just could not let himself think of her at all, because it seemed to be just too painful to think of her mother. Needless to say, his heart was truly heavy from his careless deed. Now he felt regrets about what he had done to her.

"Jamie, this is our daughter Lorramie." Frankie replied, as he broke in to Jamie's thoughts. "You do remember her, for sure, don't you?" Yes, Jamie remembered Lorramie when she was just a baby. She too played a special part in his life with Lorraine. In his mind, he pictured two small babies lying in the hospital nursery. Both of them having the name of 'Mason' at the foot of their crib. One was Timmy, a child of Jamie's and someone else. The other baby was Lorramie, which was Frankie and Lorraine's child. He remembered the awful deed that he had played on his brother, and his ex-wife Lorraine. Because he was so jealously unhappy about his brother marrying his ex-wife Lorraine, and because he had no conscience at that time, and he had a lot of money in those days, he paid the doctor to switch babies. Lorraine and Frankie didn't know the difference, because the babies was born at the same time, in the same hospital.

A year or so later the truth came out. Then Frankie and Lorraine took both of the children. However, Jamie named Lorramie after Lorraine, and him. He remembered how he loved this little girl while he had her! Now she was a dark haired young lady, and very beautiful in her own way. He was not sure just how she would feel about him now, as she should remember him. But as the guilt feelings swelled up within him again concerning her, and all the other guilty feelings that he was experiencing just lately, since the telegram came, he fortified his mind once again with a promise from the Scriptures stating; "And having made peace through the blood of His cross, by Him to reconcile all things unto Him." Yes, by Him it says, yes, by Him! Jamie thought. Yes, he forgives me! Praise God! I shall not feel ashamed or guilty no more! He thought to himself.

"You sure have grown up to be a very pretty young lady haven't you?" He said as he hugged her.

"I remember you too." She said; "You are sort of like my second dad, and I love you Uncle Jamie. But you are sure different then what I remember you to be!" She concluded.

"Yes sir!" Timmy added. "You sure surprised us!"

"It takes the young people to tell the truth like that." Jamie said as they all laughed together.

On inviting them into the house, Jamie felt a joy in his heart that had not been there in a long time. It was the joy of being reunited again with his family that he had forsakened for so many years! He loved to have them here where he made his new life. He knew that there was going to be a struggle for them all, especially for him and Dana, but he knew too that life was not always sunshine either. He had learned that these past twelve years. He also knew that it was going to take a long time and a lot of everything to gain Dana's love and respect too. However, he did have to cling to the idea that it could happen. He believed in what the Scriptures said when it said;"All things work together for the good for those who love God, and are called according to His purpose." Therefore, he took hope in believing that!

Waiting for them as they entered the old broken down mission home, was a neatly set table. Anyone could tell by the looks of it that the table itself had served many a meals. It was old, and worn too, same as the floor that it stood on. However, it had a tablecloth spread out on it that too was old and faded with time and much use. However, the tablecloth was clean and neatly pressed. The dishes, which did not match each other was laid out with care. Needless to say, the table and everthing around the room was very simple, and plain. It was obvious that there was not much money to spend even on such as simple everyday things, let lone anything else! It sure was not the pure, rich, elegance that these people knew in their home, back in Kentucky. Dana was the only one who showed a distaste when they all came into the room.

The kerosene lantern hung from the ceiling, almost directly over the table. Its light casted odd shadows all around the room. It made the place look a little errie. In a big kettle, over four-burner oil stove had something simmering in it. The steam and aroma that drifted up from the kettle smelled like chilli. Dana hoped to herself that she would not have to eat what ever was cooking. She wrinkled her nose, and made a face as she glanced over at Timmy. He winked, and licked his lips, as though to say that it was going to be good!

"Well," Jamie said, not noticing the children's comical wit. "This place must be hard for you folks to get use to, but hopefully you will be able to adjust before your visit here is up. I know you all are used to

17

more modern and better ways of living. I admit that it took me quite sometime to get use of it when I first arrived here, but I have gotten use to it, and to me it is not all that bad! Considering if you stop and realize that it is not all those material, and modern things that really counts in ones life. What counts most is the serenity that one feels inside that matters. But I do hope you all can adjust!" He calmly concluded, with a manner of politness toward them.

"This doesn't seem much like you!" Lorraine spoke up, surprising her self, and feeling a little embarrassed. Jamie smiled at her as though he could agree with her too if he stopped to think about how he use to like to live in his past, but he also was trying to make her feel at ease for what she had said.

As they talked concerning the things that had happened back home in Kentucky, Nadine came in carrying a pail of cold water. Jamie immediately went and took the pail from her, and set it up on the sink board. He then turned to Nadine, and put his arms across her shoulders. He was silently letting her know that he appreciated her.

"Folks, I want you to meet Nadine." He said in a loving and proud way. She wondered if he had changed his mind about telling them about her. She looked at him with a big smile. "Yes, this is the gal that always manages to do the right things""

As Nadine heard Jamie talk, and he said no more concerning them, she just smiled at these strange people, and they then smiled back, and said it was really nice meeting her. She then went back to the things that she was doing, like putting supper on the table. She wanted to find out more about her husband's past life. She was thinking about the strange people that had just arrived. She wondered if she could ever fit into the picture. She wondered if these people would make Jamie change. She wondered if his feelings for her would change too. She also wondered if she did the right thing by being so trusting of him. She wondered why she herself was so willing to stay in the background concerning this situation, but all she could do now was to wait, and see just what would happen. She knew that the only answer to her questions now was now in her future, and she felt that she had to trust Jamie, and her God.

"CATCHING UP ON ALL THE NEWS BACK HOME" CHAPTER 4

At the table there was much talking going on. Jamie learned some things about the children and their plans for their future. Timmy thought that he would like to be come a baseball player like his dad was at one time. He was very good at pitching. But yet he really wasn't too sure that that was what he really wanted to do. He sort of wanted to stay here at the mission for awhile; mainly he wanted to get to know his Father better. Jamie was very pleased to hear that his boy wanted to stay and so he tried to encourage Timmy to do so.

"What are your plans Larramie?" Questioned Jamie.

"Well first of all, I have got to finish college." She said, as she glanced over at her parents. "Just to please my dad and mom, that is!" She looked at her father and said; "Right?"

"Absolutely! I should say so!" Frankie replied in a definite voice.

"Well anyway! She giggled. "After college, then I want to sing. I really have a great voice, especially since I have had voice lessons! Tim can vouch for my singing talents, right Tim?" She said jokingly, looking at Timmy for his comment.

"Oh yes!" He said teasingly. "She hit such a high note once that it shattered the big picture window in the living room!"

"If my memory serves me right, I think that it was a baseball that went through that window, wasn't it" Inquired Lorraine.

"I don't know what, or who caused it to shatter into bits," Laughed Frankie, "But it cost enough to replace it, I know!" Then they all laughed.

"Well what is your future plans Dana?" Jamie asked his daughter, in hopes that it too might include staying on here for a while. "Do you have any plans yet?"

Everybody looked at Dana, and waited for her to answer. It sort of took her off guard, for she had been hoping that her dad would not ask her. She answered with a quick and short reply. Her face turned a rosy red, for the surprised attention that was put uponher.

"Oh, I do not make plans! I am still in school yet!" She said in a matter of fact way.

"Danny isn't sure." Lorraine broke in trying to relax Dana a little. "A very few things has caught her interest yet." Lorraine's reply helped Dana to add more.

"Well I guess I just want to finish school, and get married. I would like to have a home." Dana said politely, after she went back to her normal pose, for her face had turned rosy red again as she looked directly at her father. The both of them acted a little embarrassed. Jamie put his head down as she continued.

"I, well I guess I would like to be a wife, and a mother someday, that is all.

But there is lots of time for that too, I guess. So I really do not think too much about it now." She put her head down, and then concluded." Try to keep in mind what Aunt Lorraine tells me, and that is that all good things usually comes slow. I guess I can wait a little longer." Jamie took a quick glance at Lorraine, then nodded with his approval.

After supper was finished, and the dishes was all cleared away with the fast work of Nadine, for she went right at the job to get it done as she was to use to doing. She worked quietly, and efficiently. In the mean while, the rest went out to the veranda to try to get some relief from the heat that still hung over heavy, even thought the sun had gone down hours ago. Nadine lingered in the kitchen. Her thoughts was about her husband, his family. She thought of the two of them, and how would she ever fit into his type of family. She even entertained the thoughts that

Jamie seemed different toward her since they had arrived. She thought of how little she really did not know about her husband's past . For the time being she felt unsure about her man. She knew that Dana and Timmy was really Jamie's children, and she wondered about who their mother was. She thought that perhaps she had been too trust worthy concerning his love. As she stopped and thought about it, she was amazed as to how many times since she heard about Jamie's family, that she felt so unsure about him! She, on thinking about it, felt despair set in, and she sort of wished that Marleiny and the rest of their children was home , then things would have to be delt with in a different way then it was. This situation worried her , and she tried really hard to listen to what Jamie, and the strangers was talking about. She was thinking and hoping that she might just get somekind of a clue or something that would let her know a little bit more of what was going on. She thought to herself that she must not let Jamie see her distrust in him. He had always been such a good husband, and a good father that she resolved to continue her trust in him a little bit longer. But she mostly was gonna put her trust in her great God above, who knew Jamie's heart, and would help him to deal rightly concerning these things. God had never let either of them down yet!

Differrent sounds came from the far off darkness, as the kids sat down on the steps together. They whispered softly together, while their parents set at the far end of the veranda.

"Do you think that you will stay on here?" Questioned Lorramie.

"Do you think we should?" Was Timmy's reply.

"I do not know if I really want too!" Dana said. "This is sure a weird, and errie looking place!"

"You can not fo by that." Timmy replied in a calm voice, as his father would have.

"It sure is gonna be hard to get use to! At least I would find it sort of hard." Said Lorramie.

"Oh you girls just do not have very much adventure spirit in you, that is for sure!" Joked Timmy, "True, I surpose that there is no hair salons here, or Country Clubs, or those big Maga-Malls that you girls love so much to spend your time and money at, but what is such a big deal about them anyways?"

"I bet that there is no money to spend on those type of things here either, if there did happen to be any around!" Exclaimed Dana.

"I bet there isn't either!" Exclaimed Dana.

"Yes, but you know that money is not everything, either is all that other stuff that makes you girls happy ." Interrupted Timmy, feeling that he had to defend his father in some way.

"No, but it sure helps!" Chorused the girls. Timmy just gave them a discusted look, and shook his head.

The adults had just nicely got seated when Jamie asked.

"Well what is going on back home? Is there anything that I should hear about?" Questioned Jamie. "What is the old gang doing since I left? Go ahead fill me all in on akk those twelve years that I have been gone."

Lorraine laughed as she leaned back on the porch swing. The big fan that was directly over them, turned tremendously in an attempt to cool the warm air that dominated the night.

"Things has changed, Jamie!" She sighed.

"Well, not really." Frankie interrupted her. "They are still all having their problems! Kelly never really did find, according to my way of thinking, her real fulfillment in life."

Yes, I guess we all were mixed up at one time or another." Said Lorraine; "I feel we all never really knew just what we wanted."

At this comment, Frankie gave her a glare, but she ignored him continue to talk.

"But you know Kelly, she always cared for steve, and I guess he knew it! Only his love for her was not as right for either of them. He really needed the type of woman that Diane was, to depend on. But Kelly, and steve did not seem to be able to stay away from each other."

"I guess a lot of people are like that." Frankie said, with a sort of sarcastic tone in his voice. Lorraine gave him a disapproving look, but kept on talking to Jamie as though Frankie had not said anything.

"Well anyway!" She continued. "This sent Tommy to drinking! I never did think that Kelly, and Tommy's marriage would work out. I never thought that they was right for each other."

"Who is to say?" Frankie cut in agian. "There was a lot of folks that got together that I did not think was right for each other, but you could not make them see that!"

"Well darling, "Lorraine teased. "You was just the same way. You was not so sure just what you wanted out of life there for awhile either."

"I always knew who I wanted!" He said with a positive voice.

"Ya, just to do a little researching in your behalf," Kidded Jamie; "You sure had it bad for a woman named Morgan once, remember?"

"A woman named Morgan!" Frankie muttered with a slight embarrassment when he thought about her, then in a teasingly way, he said: "I wonder if she would go for me now?"

"Just forget it old boy, your future is already been mapped out for you. I have already staked my claim on you by now!" Lorraine laughed.

"For a long time Steve was seeing Kelly." Frankie said, going back to the subject of Steve and kelly, as though he was seeing Kelly." Frankie said, going back to the subject of Steve and kelly, as though he was changing the subject of him and Morgan. "And Tommy tried to make time with Diane. As you remember right, they too had this thing going between each other once. Well at least tommy thought so!" Jamie nodded in agreement as he himself recalled those days back at Woodgate, Kentucky, and the old gang.

"But anyway, Diane did not intend to let Steve slip away that easy. He was such a catch anyway!" Frankie joked.

"Well I use to think that he was sort of charming, in his own bashful way!" Replied Lorraine. "I always liked his tall slim shape, in those tight fitting jeans, and his deep voice was so captivating!"

"Will you stop thinking about that cowboy Steve, and let me tell it my way dear?" Frankie asked Lorriane, all the while trying not to let on that it really was bothering him on what she was saying. On seeing a little friction between his brother and his brother's wife, Jamie broke in on the coversation.

"But I always believed that Diane loved Steve in a very special way. At least that is how I always saw it. Well what happen then?" Steve was a very close friend of Jamie's once, and he was really interested in how life was going for him. Steve was Merle's brother, and diane was Jamie's sister, so that made them extra good friends. Well Frankie contiued talking.

"Well Diane really did love Steve, at least that is how it came across to me.

If only he had realized that! But he did have some sort of a complex, of problem, in how he was, and how he believed. It was probably the way he was brought up, but anyway he stayed kinda like a mystery to everyone, even probably to his wife too! Who knows what has happend to him to have him be such as he is? He did a lot of traveling all over the country playing in rodeo!"

"Ya," Added Lorraine; "And Kelly always managed to be there too. They saw a lot of each other. Then Diane got a plan that changed things! She knew she had to do something drastic inoder to get Steve's attention, so she too, joined the rodeos. Of course this bothered Steve big time! And him Diana got into some pretty hot arguments together. He thought that she was trying to show him up on the work that he had gotten so good at. He felt that she was threatening his manhood I guess. Anyway he had to leave Kelly on the sidelines while he battled it out with Diane. Well as a lot of arguments go, they called a truce, and made up and went back together again I guess they realized how much they meant to each other. I can see Steve now, with that big cigar in his mouth, and his hat pulled down so far that you could not look him straight in the eyes!" Lorraine laughed; Then they all thought it was funny when they stopped and pictured Steve, and the way she discribed him.

"Hey always was a weak-knee type of a guy!" Joked Frankie.

"He was not!" Lorraine quickly came to steve's defense. "He just had two woman who loved him, and in a sense I believe he learned to love each of them in their own ways. I see nothing so weak-kneed about that!"

"Can that be done big brother?" Frankie questioned Jamie. "Is it possible to love two people at the same time?"

"I don't know. Why do you ask me that?" Came back Jamie's reply.

"Well I just thought you might know about things like that!"

"I am sorry that I can not answer your question, I guess I am still tring to figure that out myself. But I do believe that it is possible. Especially the way your wife discribed it."

"Poor Kelly," Lorraine went on; "She went and joined the peace-corps after that."

There was a little space of silence after that, and they could hear the children that was still setting on the veranda steps. They was whispering back, and forth to each other, keeping their talks, and laughter down so that the adults could talk. Then Frankie broke the silence again.

"Say, you just ought to go visit Rocky, and bonny." As he laughed. "That is if you think you could keep your self from laughing your self silly! I can not even think about them, without laughing right out loud!"

"Well knowing Rocky as I do, I am afraid to ask you why, but here goes, what is with them?" Jamie said grinning, for he remembered his friends, and already knew how funny Rocky could be! That was Rocky! That was just Rock's Irish way, being funny!

"I bet you could never guess how many kids him and Bonny has, and how many are boys?" Frankie asked.

"I have no idea!" Replied Jamie; "How many?"

"They have twelve big boys! Can you imagine twelve Rockies around? the only one who acts anything like his mother, is the oldest one, Buddy. He has a calm gently way about him, that the rest does not have! But anyway, they are so comical! I just have to go see them ever so often, because it is so hirarious to see them! Bonny being just four feet something, and tiny, and then she is the mother to these over grown boys, who is at least six feet or more, even the youngest is getting taller ! Bonny is such a fussy type of person anyway, and she has such a hard time keeping them guys all in their places, but she manages quite well! Tucson gives them the most trouble. He can find more trouble to get into then twenty rebles can! But with a name like that, I do not blame him! They are all named after a town or a city in and around Texas, except for Buddy, which was probably born before all this name thing got started. Anyways, Bonny manages pretty fair, like I said, but when Rock gets one of his so called celebrations agoing, and he gets his whiskey out, even the boys get to enjoy that! By the time Rocky has got a few down him, he dose not know just who is drinking and who isn't. I think he cares less then. Poor Bonny, she tries to keep him straight, and sober too, but she sure has a lot to deal with, and I guess that it has just become their way of life! They do not feel bad, or even feel it is wrong, because that is how they were brought up to think, I guess."

"Ya, I guess that is the way Rocky has always been. He has always called it rough and rowdy', but you know, it is sad to think just how things could turn out for him in that respect. To me, he was always a very special type of guy." Then Jamie's thoughts turn to Rocky. He remebered the part that Rocky, and Bonny played in his life. Rocky was his very best friend, and constant confidnet sidekick. He always seemed to be by Jamie's side when Jamie needed a friend. Many time he was there when he did not need anyone! It seemed that Rocky always carried with him a big 'rowdy good time', and even when things was going down dulls street for Jamie, Rocky could, and would make it all interesting for him. His celebrations had always turned out, in the past, to be fun and adventurious. Even though Jamie was not always in the mood for Rocky's craziness, he could not help from having some very good thoughts of his beloved friend. Rocky was Steve's long lost twin brother, which was seperated from birth, and that made Merle Rock's sister too. Jamie had to admit to himself, that there always was, and always will ramain a special bond between himself, and Rocky, regardless how crazy Rocky became.

"By the way, Rocky is always talking about the time when he comes to hunting you down, and finding you. He never would consider the fact that you where dead, and never would come back." Frankie told Jamie; "As Rocky puts it, we will all have a big celebration, with all the trimmings, when Jam comes back!"

"And you know what all that consist of you don't you?" Laughed Lorraine.

"I guess I do know all too well!" Jamie replied, shaking his head, as he recalled those 'celebration' times. "I am really surprised that he has waited this long to find me!" Jamie said in wonderment.

"I think he started out to find you several times, but got side tracked in some all night joint." Frankie laughed. "But some time in the very near future, I guarantee, when you least expect it, you will get a knock on your door, and when you go to open it, he will be standing there, with some celebrations in his pocket." They all laughed, as they tried to vision Rocky standing there waiting for Jamie to open the door to his craziness!

Lorraine yawned, and then sighed, as though she just realized how tired the long trip made her.

"Oh, your getting tired arn't you?" Jamie asked, not realizing how tired they could be from their long trip. "I will call Nadine, if she has not left yet. She will show you where you may sleep. Nadine?" Jamie called. Nadine came quietly to the door.

"Yes Jamie? Did you call me?"

"I was wondering if you would care to help me a little bit more before you leave?" Jamie said, as he gave her a smile that was so familar to her.

"Yes Jamie, you know that I would be more then glad too!" Replied Nadine, as she smiled back at him. Lorraine watched the two talking. She too, recognized that smile! It was that same type of smile that Jamie use to give her when he was trying to assure her of his love for her. As Jamie went on to ask Nadine to show Lorraine, and the children where they was to sleep, and she assured him that she would take care of everything. Lorraine could not help but remember just how it was when she and him was together! Even though Jamie had, in the past, made a big mess of her life, she found that he was still irresistable to her. She had sort of felt uncomfortable since she had arrived here, about her feelings toward him, but thought that it would go away once she got use to seeing him again, and the situation here, but the minute she saw'that look' between Jamie and Nadine, once again she felt that feeling of love for him that she knew so well! that feeling that she knew had never really died within her. Facing reality right then, she knew that as long as she lived, that she would always feel this love for Jamie. She looked at the Indian woman, and wondered just what was so special about her, in her 'common dressed apparel', that made her deserve that 'special llok' of love! she had never seen him look that way at anyone other then her! Not even Merle knew that look, she thought.

She found herself staring right at Jamie as though she was telling him that he had betrayed the love that they once both thought was so special. Now Jamie too felt that once again, that love toward Lorraine, as he noticed the way she was staring at him, and he could not help himself, he stared back in the same way. He felt uncomfortable about how his heart raced within his chest, it was as though that it wanted to escape from these feelings that he felt for her at that moment. It

27

got worst! He felt his face get hot from embarrassment, for allowing this old feeling to come back, and over take him. Knowing all too well about this feeling, he immediately looked at Nadine again, and tried to focus on her! But as he did this, she did not smile for him, instead, she gave him a look of sympathy, for now she knew that Lorraine was very important to him! Could she be the mother to his children? She asked herself. Jamie just tutned away quickly from both woman. He did not look again at either of them again, but he spoke while gazing into the dark night.

"You must be pretty tired from the long ride!" He said again, in a nervous voice. "Nadine, will you please show Lorraine to her room?"

"I guess I will retire now. You men may have a lot to talk about yet, that is that does not concern me. So I will just say good night." Lorraine turned to Frankie, who now was leaned over with his head resting in his hands. "Come darling, when you get around to it, okay?"

"I will be there shortly." Frankie said, as he looked up at her, and reached his hand to meet hers. They kissed a formal type kiss, and Jamie stayed still, and did not look back from the darkness, until they finished, but when he did, she intentionally gave him one more long stare, and then she turned and followed Nadine into the house. The children called out their good nights too, and followed the woman inside the house.

Jamie once agian watched the two woman go into the house together, and absentmindedly nodded to the children as they said good night. He knew that he had some feelings that he needed to deal with concerning Lorraine. He knew that he had failed wickedly, that big test of loyalty! He thought about the scene that he had just displayed in front of everybody. He could not seem to have helped himself. He had thought that everything was under control! He thought that because he had sit the evening visiting with her, and Frankie, that he had nothing to worry about, but he lost all control the minute when his and Lorraine's eyes met. That was the moment his emotions went all out of control! It was like trying to hide a bad rash, or something like that. He was afraid of his feelings at that time! He worried about what Nadine was thinking. He knew that he should have went right to her there and then and tell her that he loved her dearly, and that she was something special to him, and that their life together was something far more different then any love that he had ever experienced before, by anyone else, not even children's mothers. But of course she did not know those things concerning his past, for he has never told her before this! Perplexity filled his whole being, and he felt as though he had reached the worst since he had been here at the mission. He then turned to his brother Frankie. Frankie sat back in his chair, and he had a sullen look on his face, the same look that he use to get when he was a kid, and things did not go right for him.

"Well, tell me Frankie..." Jamie started to say, trying to dirvert his brother's mind from the scene that was just before his eyes. He was hoping that his brother had not taken too much notice of Lorraine, and him.

"Blast it all anyway!" Frankie bursted out. "It never cease to amaze me! You two made that pretty loud, and clear to me! Blast I hope you go to hell someday for your way of thinking!" He got up from his chair, and walked over to the porch railings. He also started off into the darkness for a long time. Jamie just watched his brother. He was thinking his brother's words through, and was wondering just how he should respond to them, or if at all. He knew that Frankie was mad enough to punch him out of his mind, and in a way, he would not have blamed him, and sort of wished that he would. He felt that it was something that Frankie had held back for a good many years anyways. He thought that if he did, then it would make Jamie feel more justified about what had happened. Not just what happend tonight but this conflict that has been going on so long about both of their feelings concerning Lorraine. It seemed that Frankie had always tolerated him from day one! Frankie would slam him with insults, but he has always quite there! As Jamie was searching for the right words to say, Frankie spoke up.

"You know it is so funny!" He said, hitting his fist in to the palm of his hand as though he really wanted to hit somebody, namely, his brother.

"What do you mean? I am not sure I follow you!" Jamie said slowly, even though deep down in his gutts, he knew that Frankie was not talking about something that could be laughed at. Actually he did not really want to know what Frankie was talking about. He knew that it couldn't be good, but he impulsively, he asked agian.

"So what is funny?"

"You and her! My wife, and you!" Frankie made a jester toward the door where the women went. "No, better yet, about you and every other woman across this continent!" Turning back to Jamie, he flew his hands up in the air in discust.

"I should have know better then to bring her here! I should of known that it was still the same between you two! It will never change! You and her will never get over each other! Why should it bother me so bad? It will never change! Never!" He repeated the words. "I never really had her! I might as well give her up to you right now!"

"But you have got it all wrong!" Jamie protested. Frankie just shook his head no. No! He did not have anything wrong! He saw what he saw!

"You saw it all wrong Jamie protested again. "I will admit I sort of got taken back into the years, and showed some emotions for a few minutes, but it was just a natural human reaction that you saw. You just saw something that you knew yourself that you would see, at some time or another while you was here. You expected it! You still have fear, and guilt feelings for taking her away from me once, and because of it, you look for anything that will make you feel right and justified for doing so. Lorraince and I really cared about each other at one time, and we just acted two people would who had shared as much as we have together! But I sware, it was just emotions! You have had her at least seventeen or more years since I was in the picture. She loves you, but she needs some kind of closer! Well I guess possibly I do to concerning her, but I do not love Lorraine as you do now! You have this all wrong! As far as ever changing this 'electifying feelings' between us, the feelings that brought us together in the first place, before you came into the picture, well I can not say that it will ever go away! I know I would be lying to you if I did say it would! But I can say, give me a chance, and I can keep it under control! Yes, for a few minutes there was that old feeling between us, but I can say, it is not real love! It never was, and it never will be ever, because we have come too far, too much has happend that has killed true love in the bud. It never got the chance to blossom in the right way. It never was, it never will be, because me and her never gave it a chance. We never nourished it to become real. It is just a feeling, an emotion for now ma appear alive, but will fade out in the years to come, and just become faint memory of something that never could be good ." Jamie concluded.

Frankie sat back down on the swing, and he laid back his head, and stared up at the fan. It was spinning in circles, and it seemed to him that the fan was like brother, in a sense that it keeps on turning just to cool the air, but the air still remains so hot. It keeps going, around, and around, trying hard to get somewheres, but it still ends up back in the same place where it started! It is still spinning and still doing no good! At least that is how it seemed to Frankie. Just taking up the big space on the ceiling, using up oil, and all in all it could be replaced with an electric, and it would do more good then what was there taking up space! It was true that Frankie just did not see where Jamie had changes from running away from his home, and family, and all the responsibilities that he left behind. It all seemed so stupid, and hopeless to Frankie at this time.

It was true that he had his sights on Lorraine from the first time he ever saw her with Jamie. And he worked really hard to get her to recognie that he was someone besides just Jamie's younger brother. He felt in a way, that he was from a better stock then Jamie was! He was the one who stuck by her after the accident, when she really needed someone. God knows that Jamie was not there for her, he only wanted to 'win' her! It seemed to him, that Jamie always played this game of 'who can I play this game with, and whan can I get out of it? It was true he stoled Lorraine away from Jamie, and he can still feel the sweet taste of victory when she finally started to notice him. But, he guessed, the part that he failed to see was that she was on the rebound from breaking up with Jamie, and because he was so nice to her that she turned to him for comfort. Just, at the same time, and same reason, that Jamie turned to Merle, when they first met. Jamie is not the guilty one here! He himself is!

How many times since he married Lorraine, that he caught her staring off into space, and her mind was being preoccupied by something that she would only label as; 'Oh it is just nothing really,' or 'I am just tired!' when all along he knew that his brother Jamie had made a visit to Lorraine's memories! He could not even count the times that he lay right next to her in bed, and she would think that he was sleeping, and then she would cry softly to her self, thinking he did not hear. Many times she has called out Jamie's name in her sleep! All along he knew, even though he did not want to admit it to him self, but she was grieving over the great loss of losing Jamie after he disappeared! He wondered to him self just how many other women felt that way about his brother! While Frankie was hashing this all out in his mind, there remained silence between the two brothers; for you see Jamie was doing a lot of thinking of his own. Then suddenly, Jamie jumped to his feet, and went over to the railing of the veranda, Jamie's sudden movement startled Frankie out of his thoughts.

"What is the matter?" Frankie asked.

"Listen! Do you hear those drums?" Questioned Jamie.

Frankie had heard the drums a short time before, but he didn't really take note about them as anything serious. His life was made up of music, and of course drums, so he subconsciously gave them no thought. But to Jamie, from living among many heathens, knew that it meant serious consequences for some poor soul. He could tell the different ritual that was being performed, just by the different sounds that the drums made.

"Yes, but what does that mean?" Frankie casually asked.

"Those drums mean that there is trouble!"

"Trouble? What kind of trouble?" Frankie still could not understand what kind of trouble that just playing drums could cause.

"It means that there is a ritual going on by the heathen natives there. It is a satanic ritual, where there is going to be possibly a human sacrifice, most likely a baby! It just depends on what the natives are upset from! They believe if they offer a human sacrifice to their heathen gods so then all will go well with their tribe!" Jamie explained.

"Do they still do things like that now day? Why it is not right! Frankie said in surprise! "What can we do to prevent it?" In his mind, he was thinking that there was a fast solution to it, that they could do.

"There is nothing that we can do, except educate these people of the gospel. We have to show them that it is not right to take an innocent life. We have to show them that what goes around comes around. If they take a life, then they automatically have their life taken too. Maybe not right off, but everything must make a full circle, it is just the way nature works! That my brother is my work here! I am here to bring these heathen natives to their Saviour!" When Jamie talked like this, there seemed to be something that penetrated through Frankie's mind, and a wonderful, peaceful feeling took over within him. He never saw his brother in this sort of light. Something about Jamie seemed new and different, and to Frankie, it felt refreshing.

Frankie did not say no more. Even though his brother might be judged wrong by him, it did not change the fact that Lorraine still had issues, or feelings to deal with. There was still that long stare that had to be delt with! It was not the stare alone, but the feelings that was behind that stare. Just what feelings between his wife, and his brother, made them all hot and bothered, just by looking at each other? He thought that if they really still cared for each other yet, then not even Jamie's Christian sincerity would change them feelings that remained dormant there. He felt that if she went back home while still having these feelings for Jamie, that she would never be settled, or happy with him. As much as it hurt him to think about it, he knew in his heart, that she would have to prove to herself that there was no love left there. She would have to see for herself that it was not there anymore, and it was just a natural reaction for them to have these feelings, because of their past life together. They both would have to see that it was like Jamie had said, just a natural reaction.

Frankie was not too sure just how things would turn out concerning him, his wife, and his brother, but he knew that life could not go on as it had been. He knew that some one had to prove some thing, if no more then him self who had to do it! He had lived with this thing much too long. That was one reason why he came on this visit, was to find out the truth of the matter!

Just then the distance drums got louder, and his mind came back to his brother again, and he asked this question.

"Is this where you want Dana to be brought up in? Is this the kind of life that you wish for her? Do you really want to take her from a nice comfortable home, and bring her in this God-forsaken country?" He did not finish all that he wanted to say.

"But you see, God has not forsaken this country! That is why He sent people like me, the missionaries, here to show this country, and these people that He has not forgotten them!" Jamie said in God's defense.

"I mean to say! Is this the place you want Dana to live in?"

"Well what does she feel?" Questioned Jamie, not wanting her to stay if she could not be happy here. "Does she think as you do? Does she think of me as a worthless no good father who lives in a God-forsaken country? What have you and Lorraine taught her about me?"

"Oh you can bet your last dollar that it was nothing but the best that she was taught!" He paused, "Nothing but the best! Lorraine saw to that!"

There was silence. Frankie looked at his big brother. This here was his own flesh, and blood, and he really loved him. He never really wanted to ever hurt him. He was not thinking about Jamie's questions about Dana any more, but he was thinking about Lorraine, because hearing her name mentioned reminded him once again of the subject that was at hand just before the distance drums came up on the scene. He once again knew that he had to come up with a plan to solve the problems concerning his wife, and his brother. He just had to know, regardless what happened just where the three of them stood in this crazy triangle!

"Well what about Dana?" Questioned Jamie again, for he was waiting for a reply from his brother.

"Okay big brother, this is how it appears! You know that you didn't leave much for her to cling to. And of course you're no stranger to gossip that spreads like wildfire!" Frankie was answering his brother, but still had his thoughts on how to handle this thing about Lorraine. He knew that Dana really came prepared to stay at least for a while, but he kind of wanted Jamie to feel a little anguish, for causing Dana, and the rest the anguish that they felt after he had skipped off to no-body knew where!

"It is hard for her to think rightly about you. It was not so bad when she was just little, but she certainly not a little girl anymore! She feels sort of hostile toward you, even though she doesn't think she does. We really tried, especially Lorraine. Yes, Lorraine really tried to keep your memory alive for Dana, and herself! Lorraine never would believe that you was dead! We tried to bring her up to love you even as we loved you, but we had very little to go on. Timmy helped a lot. Although he was always talking about the good times that he remembered, I wondered even where he got them from! It appears to me now, that that thing you said about the natives, about what goes around comes around, is some what happening to you right now! Now that I see just how you live, that it is going to be your turn to suffer a little bit, for it is going to take a lot, I believe, to for you to win her back!" He was still adding living a little bit, but he felt that his brother needed a little adjusting to the facts too!

"Well I really love Dana!" Jamie said briskly, his voice holding a strange intensity. "But I will let her choose as she pleases! Because this is no place to be for some one who does not want to be here! Dana is at an age of understanding and she surely knows where she would rather be! Would it be here, or...?" His voice felt the lump forming in his throat, and it tapered off, and he just could not finish. He just sat down and put his head in his hands.

"Oh yes! You take that easy way out brother! Just like you did the last time that you did not get your way! I thought you had learned, as a preacher of the Gospel, how to give love unconditionally!" Frankie came back at his brother in full force! "Yes, you take that route, and then it won't mess up your life! Never mind about that tiny helpless baby that you so graciously turned your back, and walked out twelve years ago. Of course she is old enough to speak, and made decisions by her self! Never mind about fighting for her, and showing there is some love, at least you could come up with the sort of love you would have for a everyday sinner, she would be happy with any kind of love from you!" Frankie really lost his temper, he was very upset with Jamie's attitude toward Dana staying, or going. Frankie went on;

"We hoped that this trip would change her mind about you. Just maybe it will! But I am wondering now, it depends you! It has been a hard long twelve years since you turned your back on her you know. I have to ask this, what to hell was you thinking of that day you left that tiny little baby in her crib all by her self? You did not even think about any body except your self that day! Lucky for Dana some one who loved her was keeping track of you both! You did not leave her much, or if anything at all! You know you are my big brother, and I love you dearly, but I still am angry at you for doing that dirty deed to her! You left her, and a house full of memories. Memories of a very sweet mother, and memories of a very careless, and reckless father! Now you want her to just forgive and forget, just because you have learned to do that!It is still in your terms! Imagine that! She is surpose to come down here and live here, or go back as she pleases! She still is surpose to love you as though you have never ever left her behind. Man! Big brother, what made you do that to your children? Regardless what ever your excuse was for leaving the way you did, why? Tell me what is so different between those babies that are being used for sacrifice, and you leaving your brand new newborn lying all alone in her crib? And why did you want us to think that you were dead? You know man, you may feel right with your God, but you had better get to feeling right about your children too. They both need answers, and the truth for a change! Infact we all do! I need to know myself why?" Frankie took a deep breath and Jamie just kept his head down.

"You know, we still would not know where you are, or if you was even alive, but I figured I had to know, and I hired a private detective to hunt you down. Dana has been miserable all her young life just because she thought that you did not want her. There were several reasons why we made this trip, but one was that we hoped that it would help her change her way of thinking about you!" Frankie went on; "It has been a hard twelve years! You probably know this by now, because I keep repeating it, but to stress the fact that you did wrong, and messed up big time back then! That is why I keep repeating it! You preachers, and I mean to show you respect, but you are always talking about the day of reckoning, well your day is here in the now!If you fail your children now, it is likely to be your last chance, because they are getting older, and soon they won't be needing you! So I say it here and now, you have a short time to make it right with those children of yours, because if you do fail them now, I swear to God you will never get the chance again as long as I live!"

Jamie hurt badly inside. He knew that Frankie was saying this because it was true, and also because Frankie really loved him. He had not, and would not ever leave his four little ones that were away visiting their aunt, and he knew that he could not ever treat them as he had Timmy, and Dana. Infact he missed them so much that it seemed as though he could not stand it until they returned home, but he never ever took the time to even think and remember Timmy, and Dana! What made the difference? What made him do such a thing to them? What was he thinking all those years? What made him so very selfish? How could he have been such a person? On thinking about all this, he could not blame Frankie for not trusting him either! Why should he? He was such a rat once! Why should anyone think that he had a changed from what he once was?

With feelings of exhaustion, both brothers stood up, and Jamie put his arms around Frankie's shoulders. This was his little brother that use to put up with anything that he did and always tried to find excuses for it. Frankie stood tall in frame, and in manhood. He knew that Frankie deserved a lot of thanks, and respect from him.

"Frankie," He said seriously, "Will you please try to forgive me for all that I have done to you, Lorraine, and the children in the past? You have always had a lot of faith in me, even when I did not deserve it. Well once again, I am asking you to please believe in me again, for this time I deserve it. Please do not lose that faith that you had in me now after all this time! Please just judge me from now on, better yet, try not to judge me at all! Just leave that up to God. I promise I will do my best not to disappoint either of you. But please stand by me if I do fail to measure up to your expectations!" He dropped his arm from Frankie's shoulders,

"I will try brother! I will try!" Frankie said with a big smile.

Dorothy LaRock Skinner

"A RESTLESS NIGHT FOR JAMIE" CHAPTER 5

That night Jamie did not go to his bed. He felt he just could not sleep. He had too much to think, and pray about. After what happen between Lorraine and him, and to add to that, all that Frankie had said to him, made him feel weak, and weary. It made his mind whirl with a lot of things. He had made such a mess of things in his life time. He had hurt so many people! How could he feel any worth to any one now? He knew that he was now reaping all the things that he had sown into his life. All that bad seed was now growing up in maturity, and was starting to choke out his renewed life that he had found here at the mission.

At the time that he had sown all those bad seeds, he never once stopped and thought about it all coming back to him. Not once! Who does? Nobody! He thought of Timmy, and Dana. He knew that he loved them both very much, but he also knew that it would have been just a little bit easier for them to love him, had he lived a better, and more responsible life in his past. Considering all that he had been, and done, he couldn't blame them one bit if they never came back to him. Maybe either of them could, or would be happy living here with him at the mission. He could tell that Dana held so much against him! He felt that she never would forgive him now. But as for Timmy, he thanked God for Timmy. Timmy was such a nice gentle young man, and he seemed

39

very forgiving, and it was a good chance that he just might fit in quite well.

Putting the thoughts of the children aside, he thought about the situation concerning Lorraine and his feelings about her. He really had to admit that he was not too sure about those feelings! A part of him yearned for her arms around him, and her kisses. A part of him still lingered behind with her. How could he deal with these feelings? Would he go back into the past, and be as he use to be? How could he even think about such things?

He knew that he was such an awful person at one time. When he thought about it all, he could not blame Frankie for not trusting him. He was not even sure he could even trust himself, his feelings had proved that! Why should he expect anyone else to put their trust in him? Why would anyone that use to know him, believe that he could change from that man that they knew back twelve years ago? What he feared most at this point was just how would he feel when Lorraine stared at him again? He only had an image in his mind as to how he use to deal with such things. He knew that she had weakened him so many times, just like the feeling that he couldn't help from getting tonight when she looked right at him like she did! He wondered if the testing time would come again to him, and how would he be able to resist her? He knew her ways, all to well to misinterpret that look.

Then there was Nadine, and their children! He must never hurt them. They where his first real family and the only true one that he had ever really had! They have made up his whole life! The thought of losing them, and their love really broke him up! Just the thought made him cry out;

"Oh Father! Please help me now! Don't ever let the temptation come! But if it needs to be Thy will, for my own salvation, then please give me the strength to over come it! Please give me the victory over this!" He prayed aloud.

Now Nadine stood off in the distance, for she had seen him leave the house, and she followed him. He did not know that she was there. She stood quietly and listened to him. She did not understand just what was bothering him. She too thought about Lorraine, and the scene that had happened a few hours earlier. She felt sure that Lorraine was part of Jamie's past that he was having such a hard time to forget. She thought of how little, and beautiful Lorraine was with her red auburn hair, and she could see just how Jamie would have loved someone like her. She thought that possibly she might be Dana, and Timmy's mother. She remembered them staring at each other with emotions as though they could just run into each others arms! She saw that it was feelings that they could not help from showing, no matter how hard they tried. With that thought in her mind, she could not help from fearing for her beloved husband, and her self.

Shaking all those thoughts from her mind, she tried to pull her feelings together. She knew that she just had to trust him, for he had not ever let her down so far, and so she just had to believe that he would continue to do so. On believing this, she felt that she had to stand by him. She wanted to help him feel better. She wanted to comfort him so badly, but she still waited in the distance, because she knew that he had to first draw all his faith and strength from God. She knew that he wanted, and need these moments alone with his heavenly Father, so that God could help him get through this crisis that he was now facing. She knew that there was some sort of a bad thing concerning him, but she did not know just what. Then after some time, she finally came up softly to him.

"Just what is troubling you, my darling?" She asked, "Are your burdens heavy tonight?" She questioned, as she ran her fingers across his forehead, pushing his ruffled hair back.

"Yes." He whispered, as he held her close to him. He remembered just how bad that he wanted to hold her like this earlier, when she had turned her back on him to take Lorraine into the house. "But I must not burden you with some things that only God and I can change." As he spoke, his thoughts went right back to Lorraine again. "No!" He said at the thought of Lorraine, and the feelings that he feared so much. "No, I just can not burden you with this, my love!" At stating this, Nadine really did fear to her self that her husband did not want to share with her, as she thought that they always had, what was really bothering him so. It really hurt, and automatically she tried to encourage him to tell her.

"I realize that I do not know all about what is happening, but I am your wife. This awful thing already involves me, because it concerns you! You know that what ever hurts you hurts me! Why then, I ask, can't you just tell me all about it?" She relied.

""No! No, this is my problem!" He said quickly back to her. Jamie felt so many things concerning this situation that he was in, but most of all guilt, and shame. He really did not want her to know the struggle between right and wrong that he was now experiencing. It was as though he was standing up on a steep cliff, looking down into a grand canyon, with wild animals forcing him to jump, or be eaten up! He never told her before about all this because he just could not ever say them out loud, not even to himself. He had steered clear of the wild animals up until now, and they seem to have him cornered! Even those people, who were close to him at one time, seemed to be closing in on him! No my lady, you can not know all about this, this would only hurt you bad! He thought to himself. You must never get involved in this mess! You belong to another Jamie. A different one altogether! This Jamie that is having all this trouble is not your Jamie. He held her tight as he could while he was doing all this thinking. It was a different Jamie that use to love Lorraine, or even Merle. Another Jamie that you must not ever get to know. Suddenly he felt guilty about even his thoughts, let lone his life! He did not want to go back. Not even in his thoughts, but each time he thought, and thinking was what seem to be happening to him, he felt Lorraine close to him! Too close! So as he had done so many times before in his mind, he quickly shut the door to all this thinking! He then took a hold of Nadine's hand, and they walked over to the swing, and they sat down together facing each other.

"I love you." He whispered. "You are such an angel!" He looked at her long black hair that hung straight on her back. Her eyes were just like beads, and as black as her hair. Her skin was as though she had spent all her time out in the sun, tanned as deer hide. And as he looked at her, he thought, how I do love you!

"You know?" he said in a whisper, as he looked at her. "You do know that if God ever gave me anything good, that it would have to be you! Do you believe me?" He paused a minute, then he went on. "Well you are one of the good and positive things that are mine! I know too that you love me, and I also know that you want to help me, but there is many things in my past life that I alone have got to face with out you. I mean, I have to face these things all by myself because these things are some over coming I alone, with the help of God have to deal with. I know God and I can work it out together. Having you get involved would only blind my vision. I know I would not see this situation as I ought to. So only God can help me on this. And my sweet lady, the only way you can help me is to help me carry out the plan that we started out on. The one that we agreed on. You know what that is, it is to stay put at your friend's house, until I know more about what is going to work out. I promise you that I will never leave you, or forsake you! And I will be faithful too! So my sweet lady, please trust me some more. Please believe in me, and say many, many prayers for me! And last but not least, please take care of you self for me! Please get your rest, and don't worry about what is happening now, it, I promise will soon pass. You have to do this so we can have that baby that God is sending us!"

As Jamie walked Nadine back to her friend's house that night, they walked in silence. They both realized that this was serious, and that both of them felt the stress from it all, but they both laughed as he held her close, and kissed her good night. She left him standing there in the moon light. She went into her friend's house. He watched her disappear into the house, then he turned and walked slowly back to the mission home. He spent the rest of the night in his favorite place in a little grove near the river bed.

Dorothy LaRock Skinner

"THE NEXT DAY AFTER" CHAPTER 6

The sun came up high, bright, and hot at the Navajo mission reservation. Being located so close to the Mexican boarder, the sun seemed to get hot early. Nadine was awakened by the sound of children laughing, and playing out side the window. At first she thought that it was her own children, but when she fully opened her eyes and remembered just where she was, at her friend's home, she knew it was just the children in the streets.

The things that had happened last night ran fast through her mind. It was as though all she could do was just think about the things concerning her husband. Jamie was the first in her mind. Then she thought of his brother Frankie, and his red headed wife called Lorraine. She remembered how this woman had looked at her husband. She thought of the people that had come, without any warnings, and disturbed her and her family, mainly her husband. She felt so very restless, and uneasy. She could feel the heat that had already started to dominate the day. As she got up, and went over to look out at the children that she had heard laughing and playing in the street below her window. She felt sad, and lonely. Her feelings were also mixed up. They were in such a terrible turmoil.

"Oh Jamie darling!" She said aloud. "Oh Jamie!" She repeated. "I feel I do not know you as well as I should! What kind of a life must you have lived to be so confused, and burden now?" She asked the questions as though she could get the answer without Jamie.

Looking at the children that were running about busying them selves, she remembered when she was their age. That seemed like a long, long time ago to her now. Infact being a kid was just like being in a dream, for she wondered some times if she had always been grown up, with the family that she had now with Jamie, and their children, because that is all that mattered to her now. She remembered when she first came to the mission school. She had never heard of Jesus till then. Her parents had both died during a fever epidemic when she was just thirteen. This left her and her older siblings alone. Then came the missionaries, and took her and her siblings to the mission school. There they fed them, and cared for them. They then were taught in education by the missionaries, and they felt a Godly love from those kind of people. As she and her siblings grew older, one by one they got jobs, married, and left. They made their homes elsewhere. Thus leaving Nadine behind, for she was the youngest one. She remembered how she missed her family, and just how lonely she got without them. With nothing better to do, she stayed on at the Painted Desert Mission, and worked at the clinic just as soon as she was old enough to do so.

It was at the clinic, that she met Jamie for the first time. She recalled seeing him visiting with the sick people. He would smile at them, and that smile was different then any other smile that she had ever seen from anybody! She remembered. She remembered also how he would gently touch the sick, as he prayed for them. And in church services, he was so sincere, she thought, in the way he presented his sermons. It really made her want to know the reason why he radiated so much love, and strength toward her. She, at that time didn't really know him that well. He just made her feel the power of the Great Spirit when ever he was near. From the beginning she felt this way, and she felt at times that she just wanted to be around him all the time. She, some times, felt that she just loved him so much!

But with Jamie, it was a little different. It took him a long time to show any signs other then just being her Pastor toward her. Then one day it happened! She was heading one way down the hall of the clinic corridor with her arms full of books, and he was heading the opposite way talking to a doctor. Nadine had her mind on him and she ran right into the wall! She spilled her books, pencils, and papers all over the hall way floor! They went every which way! Right away she stooped down to pick them up, and Jamie also made a jester to help her, he too stooped down to pick them up! That was when it happened! They both reached for the same book, and their hands touched, and then her dark eyes met his eyes, and they both stared as though that was the first time that they had ever really noticed each other. They both felt the adrenalin pump through their bodies with so much force that they felt uncomfortable with each other. She had already felt this about him before, but she knew then and there that she loved this man! She also felt that she always would love him. As she thought about this she once again remembered Lorraine's look that she had when she came face to face with Jamie! She knew the feeling!

Jamie, on the other hand felt a surge of fear, for he felt that he could not let himself ever feel this way again in his life. That day, after he finished helping her pick up her books, he then walked away leaving her with out a clue as to how he felt about her. He tried hard to stay away from her. They would see each other at different times, in different circumstances, but it took him a long time to even let on that he felt anything toward her. But in the end it did happen! One day she got really sick, and she had a high fever, and he came to pray for her healing. As he laid his hand on her to be healed, he felt a conviction in his heart to let go, and express his love for her. So he did! He told her that he wanted to marry her. As he was telling her his feelings, she opened her eyes, and gave him a big smile, and then said;

"I thought that you would never ask! Yes! Yes! I will marry you! I have loved you a long time my darling!"

After that, they were a team. Their prayers together helped encourage those who were sick. It seemed that the people in that village expected them to be together as time went on.

She recalled their wedding day. It was really quite simple. They exchanged their feelings toward each other, and promised before God that they would stay faithful to each other as long as they lived! They were married in their Native American way. She felt that Jamie's love for her was new and different to him. Not that she should pride herself, but because they shared the love of Jesus, and this, she was certain that Jamie had not had kind of love in his past. It was true, she really didn't know him well, especially about his past, but she did know that he had not known Jesus very long.

She started to get dressed for the day, as her mind rewinded things back to her about the agreement her and Jamie had made about getting married. Jamie had told her that he had a past that he wanted to forget. He said that inorder for him to be able to make headway into a better future as a minister that he had to put his past behind him. He, himself believed this and that is why he put his past in the far corner of his mind, and shut a door to block it. She believed that this was good, for she felt at the time that it just didn't matter about his past as long as they continued to leave it in the past! They must look to the future, she always told him.

He did tell her that he had a daughter named Dana, of which at the time was just a baby. Also he had a son named Timmy. But he did not say who their mother was. Nadine was so young, and in love with him, and how he was now, that she did not ask any questions at all! Now she realized it might have been a mistake on her side for not asking. She had felt that Jamie was a good man, and that was all that counted. She was all dressed by now, and she hurried off to the mission home so that she could help with the morning chores. She knew that he would need her help.

The same sun came up just as hot over the mission home as it had over Nadine's friend's Hogan, and it found Jamie in his favorit place, which was a little grove near a creek. It was here that he often planned out his sermons, but mostly he got his spiritual refreshment, so to face the day. But today, it seemed different to him. His mind had gone over and over his past, and try as he might, he could not put it all out of his mind. He felt as though he had betrayed himself, and his Saviour, along with Nadine, by remembering all those things that he thought he had put out of his mind for good! Once again, the devil was accusing him of his past sins, and once again, the devil was trying to bring back the whole rotten mess of his past, by telling him that because of these things was on his mind that God had not really forgiven him at all! All these things hung heavy in his mind. He lacked the faith he needed, and so once again he prayed for strength to over come these feelings and temptations.

Finally Jamie headed back to the mission home. By the time that he arrived, Nadine had breakfast all ready, and everyone was eating, and talking about how the night had been for them, and how good they slept. The children was joking around and laughing together as they ate.

"Well I am glad to see that everybody is so happy this morning." Jamie commented, trying to act happy too. "Must be the night went well for you all."

Nadine looked up from the sink where she was getting the dish water ready to wash the breakfast dishes.

"Yes!" She said, "All is very well, and how about you?" She asked in a casual way. "Are you happy this morning?"

At Nadine's very words, Lorraine looked up at them both as though she was looking for that look she saw last night on the two of them. Jamie secretly wanted to let Nadine know that he was doing okay. Automatically he gave her that loving assured look. Once again, as Lorraine saw the way that they looked at each other, she felt the same jealously come over her. She felt her face get hot as she saw that Frankie was staring at her. She quickly excused herself, and went to her bedroom.

Frankie knew that Lorraine had been perfectly okay until Jamie had come into the room, and he knew it must be a feeling that she could not control. It must be a feeling that she still had to deal with about his brother, for it bothered her enough that she had to leave the room. Frankie sulked a bit over his cereal, while Jamie started chatting with the children, pretending that he did not notice anything wrong. Now and then, he would ask Nadine about the things that were going on in the village.

"I have a splendid idea!" Frankie blurted out, dropping his spoon into his bowl. Everybody looked at him, just waiting for him to reveal to them, his splendid idea.

"This is so very clever! What I really mean to say is, it is great!" In silence, they all looked at him.

"I would like to borrow Nadine today. I would like her to show me, and the children around this little village of Painted Desert. I have read about Monument Valley, I would like to have her tell us all about her people, and some of their traditions. How does that sound to you young ones?" He questioned. All enthused about this, he went on, "I would like to know if you would do that for us?" He asked Nadine.

"Yes! Why not? Why don't you?" Teased Timmy. "We would really like you to come along! Would you?"

Nadine looked up in surprise. She immediately glanced over at Jamie to see if he approved.

"Go ahead," Jamie encouraged; "It sounds like a good plan. Maybe you and Lorraine can get to know each other that way." Jamie said; He sort of took a deep sigh of relief, thinking that possible the test for him would be prolonged, or maybe be resolved.

"Well," Frankie Chimed in, half grinning. "I do not believe that Lorraineis feeling up to it. But do not let that make a difference! I am sure that she will not mind." Frankie turned to his brother.

"We would like to ask you to go too, but I heard that you had a lot of things to get caught up on. I thought that this would give you a chance! A chance to do what ever has to be done!"

Jamie thought that it was very clever of Frankie to think up such a splendid idea! Jamie turned away from his brother, as though he did not want to look his brother in the eyes. He did not want his brother to see his nervous reaction to the situation.

"Yes, I guess I do have some work to do, but, well you go ahead Nadine. It is okay if you join them. I will manage okay." Jamie replied, still trying to not show his true emotions about it all.

"I can imagine you will!" Frankie groaned, after Lorrammie had taken Nadine by the hand and led her off to get ready.

Words flung to Jamie's mind! They was just tugging to come out! There was things he wanted to say, but instead he choked them back. He knew that anger was not the answer. He knew it would get him no wheres!

By then Frankie excused himself, and went to his room. Jamie stood there in the kitchen, left in thought. He thought about Lorraine, and him being left home alone together. Why? He asked himself, was Frankie doing this crazy thing? He really acted like he wanted them to be alone so that something could happen!

"If I fail this test I will be proving to Frankie, and Nadine that my new life is not new at all! I will become a hypocrite!"

Will he really be able to over come these feelings that he knows he has for Lorraine? Will he prove faithful to God? Will he remain faithful to Nadine? Or will he fail them both? In his test concerning his love for Lorraine, will he have the will power to stay strong? That was the questions that he asked himself while standing there alone in his kitchen!

Dorothy LaRock Skinner

"A TIME OF TESTING"
CHAPTER 7

The house was all quite now, and only the clicking of Jamie's old typewriter could be heard. He was trying to type out his sermon. Never before had it been so hard for him to write it. He felt nerved up, and anxious about his situation. It seemed to him, like the old Jamie that was so many years ago, was tugging at his emotions, and it seemed like his old self had just awakened from a long sleep, and wanted to come out. There seemed to be two voices within him that kept talking to him in his mind. One was saying that he could never make it. That he was really hung up on Lorraine and the weakness that he felt for her would never go away, and it would win in the end!

Then there was the other voice within that kept saying to him that the battle had already been won! That he no longer needed to listen to his carnal nature. That all he had to do was call upon the name of the Lord, and resist the devil, and then these temptations would leave him alone. Now in his heart he believed that the later voice was right, but he also knew that he must be enjoying these feelings that he had for Lorraine yet, or else he would not toil over them so much! He would take the route that the Lord had taught him, and like the Bible say, "...the devil will flee from you." He thought to him self that he must like this pressure, or else he would not keep it at the top of his list that plagued his mind. Thinking, and feeling these things, he almost felt he needed a cigarette! Well at least he thought he could smell one burning!

"Well what is the matter with me anyway?" He said aloud. "I have not smoked a cigarette in years! Besides it never was anything I ever felt I needed! It was never a big habit!"

He tried to put his mind on his sermon, and his typing again, but kept making a lot of mistakes! He yanked the paper from the typewriter, and wadded it up, and threw it on the table. In discouragement, he got up from the chair, and walked over to the window, and stared out it. He wondered how Nadine was doing with his family. Visualizing her in his mind, he compared Nadine to Lorraine, and then Merle. The feelings that he felt for all three women, in its own perspective way seemed strange to him. Even so strange that he could not figure out how it could be, for he found that he loved all three of them! Possibly all in different ways, but none the less, he truly loved all three! In an attempt to efface this all from his mind, he said aloud;

"This is so crazy of me to be thinking this way! I can not possibly love three women like that! This is just plain crazy!"

He walked back over to the table, and once again, he smelt the scent of a cigarette smoke again, this time he knew it was not in his imagination, it was for real! He knew at that moment that he was not alone! Quickly turning towards the door, he came face to face with Lorraine. She was standing in the doorway. They stared at each other a long, almost seemingly endless second. Then trying to stay really calm, he slowly turned back to the table, and tried to pick up the mess that he had made with the wads of papers that he had scattered on the table.

"You came up so quietly, I did not even hear you come in to the room!" He mumbled, still keeping his head turned from her. During the few seconds that followed, he closed his eyes and silently prayed for help from this temptation that he knew would soon be there for him to over come. He knew that it was 'testing time' for him!

"Was it that I was so quiet, or was it that you were so preoccupied with all those memories of your women?" She laughed; "Care for a cigarette?" She said, as she offered him the pack.

"Oh no, no thank you anyway. I am still not much of a smoker. Remember, that was one thing that I could not get into. Being a baseball player, I needed all the clean and fresh air I could get, so I could run faster, and make all those home runs! No, I really have to stay away from bad habits that ruin one's health." He said, as he smiled at her.

"But you know," He continued; "Life is strange; it is really hard for me to believe that I am still facing a lot of those given up habits!"

Lorraine laughed at what he was so seriously trying to tell her.

"What? Am I one of your old bad habits? You seem to have an attitude toward me since I have arrived. I just do not know what you are thinking! What is it Jamie? Am I still in your thoughts? Were you thinking about us just then?" She questioned;

Now Jamie tried to evade her wonderings, answered her;

"Well I guess I am pretty busy here with my work. I have a deadline to meet." He said, as he tried to take her mind off from what she had asked. "My job still requires a lot from me, you know!"

"Yes, I bet you are pretty busy. You have really got it made here, in some sense of the word." She exclaimed. "You are way off where hardly any body really knows you, or who you really are, and you have got this lovely little Indian woman...what is her name now? Oh, Nadine, or something like that! She makes a good little mistress to you! And no one has to look twice to notice just how sweet you are with her. She is just like a little puppy following you around, catering to your every wish! Just like Merle and I did! This time you got your self a young one! She should last you a little while!" There was a long silence, then she added; "

"Did you love us all? Was that special look you use to give to me, given to us all?"

Jamie remained silent while she talked. It seemed to him that he was hearing exactly just what he expected to hear, and he hated it! She then walked over to him, and turned his face up, as a mother would do. Then she looked straight at him for a long time. All along he was feeling the pressure of this old love affair surge up within him. As her lips came close to his, a million things rushed through his mind. His heart raced with the memory of her kisses. He was now at the door step of this temptation. He had two choices. One was that he could walk in that door and enjoy all the pleasures that this moment would bring him. Yes, he could do this, and only he and her would know, or reveal it. Then there was that other self urging him to turn and run from this as fast as he could! It was telling him that only bad things could come from it all. Which way should he choose?

She put her arms around his neck, and her lips were as close as his next breath. Stop! Stop this mad thing from happening, he told himself! Nothing good can become of it now! It never worked out before, and it still will not! With this heavy on his mind, he abruptly took her hands from around his neck, and he stepped back away from her.

"Please do not do that again!" He said, pleadingly, but still with a force. With Jamie's rejections, she became hurt, and angry.

"I really want to say I hate you Jamie! I would like to say that I do not care, and that I am completely forgotten all about you! I would like to say that I do not hurt anymore concerning you! I would like to believe that I do not care what ever happens to you now!" She screamed, with tears running down her cheeks. "I would like to say all this, and really mean it, but I can not! For all my dreams are of you! Even all of my night-mares are you! At times I think I see you walking down the street, and I run to catch up, but only to find that it was not you at all! I can not stand life no longer without you Jamie!" She moved closer to him again, and slides her arms around his waist, and pulled him close to her.

"Take me in your arms right now. I am pleading with you; please kiss me like you use to do! I miss you so much! I have waited for you so long! I have searched every where for the love that we once knew!" She cried; "As far as any one will ever know…I promise you I will keep our secret always within my heart! I am yours; please make love to me once again!"

Jamie just stared at her a long time. What he felt for her, he was not sure. He only knew that there was sadness in his heart. Before him was a woman that he had always loved. He remembered just what she had meant to him. He had chased her to the far ends of the earth, just to claim her as his own! He had loved her in a way that he had never loved another, and loved every minute that he had ever spent in her arms. She had always been on his mind from the beginning, no matter who he was with! Even now with her arms around him, and her being so close, a part of him just wanted to chuck everything, and take her some where and make passionate love to her. But then there was that 'new' Jamie that just could not do that sort of thing. Even though she was begging him to take her in his arms, he just could not! Just too much to risk losing! He only felt now that he had to show her that he was not the answer to her need. There was just too much time had gone by, and just too much had happened to them both, to ever go back and be what they where once. Their worlds had turned just too many times! It was too late to go back now! He had to show her that life could still be great for her. That she did not really want to risk all she had for a short moments pleasure. He finally moved closer to her, and took the cigarette from her hand, and smudged it out in the sink near by.Turning back to her again he held her close to him, tears was running down both of their faces. As they stood there holding each other, it seemed that all the anguish drained from their bodies. They just stood there for some time just holding each other close. Then Jamie took a hold of her hand, and said;

"Come with me! Let us go out into the sunshine. Come for a walk with me. I want to talk with you about something."

Obediently, she took his hand, and followed him out the door. She was thinking to her self that soon things would be as they had always been between them. He had always returned to her, and she never could remember a time when he did not want her love. She felt that this was just another home coming for the two of them. As they walke, she admired him to her self. He is still very handsome, she thought. He is just as irresistible as he had ever been, and with joy, she thought, he is still mine, as he has always been.

Now Jamie's thoughts were something altogether different then hers. When he was holding her in his arms he made a vow to God that he would never hold her as such again. Now that he was out in the fresh air, and the sunshine, it brought him back to the reality of things better. His life that he was living for God, and his life here at the mission, with Nadine, and the young ones. He felt releived from the closness that he had felt in the house. The hugging was sort of like a healing on his part, and he silently prayed that God would keep helping him to do what had to be done. They walked until they came to a flat rock, which was inbeded in the bank of a near by river. There they sat down together.

"It is very beautiful here, Jamie!" She exclaimed.

"Do you like it here? Isn't it so peaceful? I bet you have not had your feet in a river like this in a long time! Have you?" Laughed Jamie, trying to take the things off her mind that he knew was not all that good for either of them to think on.

"Oh, it has been ages since I have even been near a river like this!" She said excitingly. "Have you?" She inquired.

"Oh yes." Jamie said seriously. "THat is where I did my washing when I first came to this country."

Lorraine laughed when Jamie told her that.

"What? You can not picture me doing something like that?" He said in a playful way, now feeling a little more relaxed at the moment.

"You just do not seem like that type to me! Now take Rocky, he might do something like that, if he thought he might get a laugh or two." She said laughing.

Her remark seemed to be like an opening to him to say what he wished for her to know. He had to get across to her just how he felt, that is when he slide his hand over hers and looked directly at her.

"As for Rocky, well he may always remain being Rocky, and doing crazy things that Rocky does." Jamie stated. "But this is the way it is with me now Lorraine. I do a lot of things now that I did not before, or would not even have thought of doing then. When you was a part of my life. But then again, there are things that I did back then, that I do not do now!" Jamie finished talking, feeling releived to think he had at least started to get things across to her as they really are. He had stared her in the eyes, when he had said what he said. He then waited for a response from her. But all he got was silence. Then just to be sure that she understood, he asked;

"Do you understand what I just said?"

Lorraine just shook her head no, as she stared back into his eyes. He then noticed tears swelling up in her eyes, and her voice began to tremble a little, as she spoke.

"No Jamie! I do not want to understand what you are saying! What you are saying is that you do not want me any more! You have got some one else to follow you around, and cater to your every wish. What you are saying is that you do not love and want me any more! If your little Indian woman friend knew that you are making a fool out of her, like you did me, would she still want you? Only I know that you have not changed! She would not know about how you have changed because she does not know how you have always been! She does not know that when you get sick of her, you will just get up and disappear! She will not know that you will be out looking for another poor little fool! Like

58

you always have! Like you did me! Like you did Merle! I know you well enough to know your entire little hang ups! Even to that sensual expression you are giving me right now!" She raged on; "This bit about you being an all fired up preacher is all make believe! I know that it is just a big cover up for you! Underneath you are still you! You are still that man with all those weaknesses! You do not fool me!"

All during her rage, she did not notice that Jamie let go of her hand, and when she finished talking, he stood up, and walked off a ways. She got right up as soon as she realized it, and followed him. He turned around and once again looked her in the eyes, as he did so, he spoke. She noticed then that he really felt terrible, for his vioce trembled, as he tried to get the words out.

"Why do people see only what they want to see?" He questioned. "I am very flattered to think that you still care enough about me to risk you happiness with Frankie, just for my love once again. But you know that flattery is only another tool of the devil's! It serves to tempt a person to sin." He paused a minute. Then continued;

"How can you stand there and tell me in one breath that you love me, and want me, then in the next breath, slam me with slander of all kinds? You are sending mixed signals! Let us face it, you love me, but you still want to hurt me, right?"

Lorraine could tell that here before her stood a changed man. A new Jamie. He spoke again.

"I guess I could care enough to love you, but, I would be selling my soul out to the devil. Like I said back at the house, for just a few minutes of pleasure, we could do it, but if you really, really love me as you say you love me, and as I love you, you would not want me to do this thing, and be lost then forever! Besides, and please think about this, you now belong to my brother, you made that choice! I did not force you to do so. I would have never let you have done that, if I would have had my say in it! But you did that on your own! Now you are his wife! It would still be wrong even if I did not belong to anyone else! But erase all else, and because the very fact that you belong to him, it would be all wrong!" He paused for a second, and wiped the sweat, and tears off his face with the back of his hand, then he took a hold of her hand again, and continued;

"It is true that you are lovelier then you have ever been, and you sure look good to me, but there is nothing on this earth so great, or ever worth the price of one's salvation! So I can not, and no matter how hard it is for me, I will not exchange mine for even a moment of my past, and that includes you! Regardless how tempting the devil makes it! I will not jeopardize what the Lord has given me. He paid a big price, His life, for me, and so I must not ever let Him down now! He paid a big price, His life, for little lost me! And so I must not ever let Him down now! I would rather die first! I really wish you could see just what I see; if you did you would feel the same way!"

Lorraine just stood there for a long time. Then she spoke up.

"If you are as you say you are, then why do you have Nadine hanging around you as you do? Any one can tell that there is something going on between you two! It is written all over your expressions, your actions! You have a relationship with this Indian woman! Do not try to deny it!" She said, in a positive way.

"Well I guess that I have to let you in about my plan now, seeing that you know that much!" He grinned. "I guess I should of came right out and been honest with you all right from the start, but I was afraid. I was afraid of how I felt about you. I was afraid that I would not be able to convince Dana that I love her. So this is what I did. But I still want you to keep this to youe self until I feel comfortable enough to let this secret out. So can you keep this little secret for awhile? You have to promise!" He asked her.

"I will try!" She answered;

"Remember now you have to keep this to your self, and do not even tell Frankie yet! Okay?"

She shook her head yes.

"Well Nadine and I are married. We have children. Four to be exact and you do not know just how it hurts me when you talk about Nadine being my mistress, but I am not blaming you. I know I should have been honest right from the start! I know that it just looks wrong to you. I guess the devil has to accuse. That is what he is, an accuser, and a lier! He likes to lay on the flattery, and when that does not work, then he has to hurt you, that way perhaps the victim will get mad, and lose their temper!"

Lorraine stood spell bound. She looked at Jamie. He spoke again.

'I love you Lorraine. I guess you will always be some one very special to me, and I can not deny that there is something very electrifying between us. I am man enough to feel it! Probably that is why we have never been able to resist each other in the past, but now I have a new will power given to me by my Saviour Jesus Christ. I can not take one step backwards, not even a minute, not for you, or for anyone else! I have love, peace, and joy that the Lord alone has given me with my new life. I am happy Lorraine; please do not take that from me! If you love me as you say you do, and it is not just passion, then love me enough to let me be at peace, and be happy. Please have some confidence in me now!"

Lorraine looked at Jamie as though she was seeing him for the first time. His eyes were not bloodshot, as they had always been charcateristic of them in the past. They where clear, and blue as she had never seen them in the past, and they where pleading with her, but not as they had in the past!

"Please!" Jamie pleaded. "Will you not join me, and my Saviour Friend? He loves you, and only He can give you the peace that you need to over come this thing, at this time!"

She looked at Jamie's earnest face, and then she glanced down by the river.

"I wonder just what it is like to wash away my sins in that river. You know I never really gave myself fully to the Lord. Maybe now is a good time. Can you baptize me? Can you make me feel at peace as you are feeling right now?" She asked in a serious tone of voice.

"Only Jesus can make you happy, but I can baptize you right now if you are sincere about this. I can baptize you right in the same river that I was baptized in!" He replied;

"Well Jesus can give you that new life right here and now. Just say that you want Him to come into your heart, and accept His righteousness, because you are a sinner. He is faithful and just, and He will give you a new life. Just sit right down there, and I will help you find your Saviour!"

Jamie said with much excitement.

Well I need to say, things went by smoothly. Lorraine and Jamie made a big effort towards forgetting their feelings about each other. Needless to say, they would always carry with them that love that they shared together, but not in the same way as they had in the past! Lorraine kept in mind what Jamie had told her about forgetting the past, and just live in the present, and look to the future.

But things did not look that good as far as Dana was concerned. Dana was not about to accept life here at the mission, so Jamie thought, it looked like to him that he had another hurtle to conquer, and unless he could conquer this, she would not be staying on.

"ABOUT DANA AND HER MOTHER"
CHAPTER 8

Early one morning before dawn, Jamie got up. He had tossed, and turned all night. It had seemed to be such a mixed up mess to him concerning Dana. Through it all, he had felt confident that the Lord would work things out if he only prayed for help, and then trusted it to be so. He knew that it would not be long before Frankie, and Lorraine would be leaving to go back to their home in Kentucky. Although he was convinced that Lorraine had accepted her Saviour, and that she had finally settled to the fact that there was no more between him and her, other then the things was to be expected, yet he still wondered about Frankie. He felt that what ever Dana decided would all depend on how his brother made her think. He could tell that Dana really looked up to, and respected Frankie about as much as she did anyone, other then Lorraine. That was to be expected, for they were the ones who brought her up! He knew that he just had to have a talk with his brother before they all left.

He thought about Dana, and what he wanted of her. But he wanted her to decide for herself. He knew it was the only way that she would be happy about it to. He wanted just what would make her the happiest. He was also thinking about Marleiny, Jeffery, Cory, and little Cherry. They where fortunately away visiting Nadine's sister, but soon they would be coming back home. By then, he would have to have his secret plan all out into the opening! He realized that perhaps it would have been much simpler had he stayed with the truth from the beginning! Had it not been for his fear about things, he would have taken that route anyway. He realized that he had lacked the faith to do the good, and up right thing! So he had taken his way, instead of God's, and the end results took him way around the bush, so to speak. Now that it is the way he thought he should do, it will take even more faith to make it right!

It seemed like he had walked a long ways from the mission house when he heard some one calling, and he turned around to see, and to his surprise, he saw Dana running to meet him. AS he watched her come closer, he wondered just how Marleiny, and Dana could ever be sisters. Their color of their hair, their complexion was like it was with him, and Frankie. He recalled the first time that he sat at the table next to his half brother, and how much difference he felt with blond hair, light blue eyes, compared to that of Frankie's, and his sister Bernadette. They both had dark eyes, and black hair. Their complexion was so much darker then his. They had been brought up so much different then he had. They had been brought like Dana. Jamie knew that Marleiny was so much different! Her life has been different, and that will make a difference between the two sisters. He knew that Frankie tried to like him, but he knew how hard it had been for Frankie to accept him, but he knew his little brother really had tried! Marleiny is two years younger then Dana, but he was sure that she would make the effort, even though he knew their lives, and ways was so different! There was so many ways of Native American life that would be, or seem to be foolish to Dana. He knew this because it was hard for him at first to get use to it. As Dana came closer, he called out to her.

"Well, it is Dana!" He said, waiting for her to come closer, and catch her breath. "What are you doing way out here so early? You should still be in bed!"

"I saw you come out here…" She said, half out of breath. She stood there, still trying to catch her breath, and breathe more smoothly. "And I wanted to have a talk with you before I went back home."

It grieved him to hear her say that she was returning back to Kentucky, but he sort of accepted that, for he did want her to choose for her self. He did not want to keep her here against her will. But he had put all this into God's hands, and felt it was up to her, and God!

"What shall we talk about?"

"My mother. I thought that we could talk about my mother!" Her voice quivered; "Just what can you tell me about her anyway?"

Jamie felt hot. The sun was not shining on him yet, but he felt anxious, and nervous, as she mentioned Merle. He turned, and gazed to the strip of sandy land, loaded with cactus plants, that lay before him. Far beyond these, was mountains, and red stone canyons, beyond that was a blue sky, touched with slight rays of early sun light. Even though Jamie knew that Merle was back in Kentucky sleeping in her dusty grave, waiting for the call of her dear Saviour, Jamie felt a closeness of her just then! In his thoughts, he felt her far beyond that Arizona blue sky! Only in memory, for Jamie there was Merle! It was like the dreams that he had dreamed of her many times! His thoughts of her and the life that they had had together came back gently like a warm summer breeze once more to steal his thoughts. Oh how he loved her at one time! He thought just how he had tried to smother her, as he had Lorraine, with his possessiveness! Oh how so selfish he had been in his so careless ways! He thought, how ironic it was, how could he feel this type of love to so many women, in so many ways? First there was Lorraine, the Merle, and now Nadine! He did not understand why it was!

Dana watched her father's eyes, and then stared off in the same direction as he did, as if she could catch a glimpse of what he was thinking. It seemed forever to her before he spoke. Finally, he did speak, and it was in a slow thoughtful manner.

"She, my dear Dana, loved me more then anyone, or anything else in the world!" Choking up some, he paused a minute, and thought, that is more then I can say for myself concerning her. Then he spoke again, for he did not want to think of just what he felt for her!

"Well, with one exception she loved her Lord more! Then it made me jealous to have her love Him more. But now!" He said, as he turned to Dana. "Now, I am happy about her loving Him more!" Their eyes met, and Dana could see tears swell upon her father's eyes.

"But, did you love her?" She mumbled, as she fumbled with a long blond curl that hung like gold on her shoulders. "What I mean is, do you still love her? I mean do you ever think about her any more?"

65

"Do you mean, is she ever thought about now? I try not to think about things that use to be. Then I was a different man, and then I am now. It is best not to live in the past. Sometimes it is best not to even try to remember. Her love for me was more then I ever deserved at that time." He said, with a matter of fact way. "I never deserved such a kind, and gentle person. I was untrue to her! I did her wrong, and hurt her right from the start! I never intended to be true to her when I married her! Maybe I should not be telling you this, but this is how it was! I learned what she meant to me when it was too late! Just too late!" He talked as though he was confessing, as though he just had just taken the lid off, and it all came tumbling out! He continued in the same manner.

"She told me Dana, that she was going to leave me. She said that she would leave me some thing that would bring me comfort. A symbol, she had said, of her love for me! I did not realize that she knew that she was going to die! I did not realize that it was you who she was going to leave me for comfort! I was too dumb to realize just what she was saying! I thought that she was just leaving me because she had found another! I thought that she had fallen for the preacher at her church!" Putting his hands on Dana's small shoulders, he faced her again.

"Yes, you know baby girl, I was too dumb to realize just what she was telling me! She was telling me that she was going to die! But she was going to leave me a part of her love with me, which was you! And you know what? I was too selfish to hang on to you! I ran from you, and stayed away, because you would only remind me of her, and how I had treated her. Now I realize, since I have the Lord living in my heart, that I want you back! I love you! But I am now afraid that you will do as I had done, and that is to turn your back on me and walk out of my life! You Dana were to be my comfort, that symbol that your mother wanted to give me. You are that which I turned my back on! I love you Dana, and I know that I have mistreated you very badly since you was born. I left you behind! I just laid you in your crib, and turned and left. At the time I was in a state of shock, but there has been twelve years that I could have changed that it some way or another but I did not want to go back! You were meant to bring me comfort, but I never gave you that chance! Now as strange as it may seem to you, I am now asking you to give me another chance. Even if you do not think I deserve it!

I have to let you make that choice! Now my sweet little girl, I have to leave it up to you to decide what you feel I deserve to get. It is your turn to turn you back on me, if that is your desire. It is up to you if you want to accept me as your father. Grant you, I would not blame you if you did not want to claim me at all! I will not force you to love me, or what I am, because that is something you, yourself will have to decide. All I can do now is pray, and wait for your decision." With pleading eyes he finished.

She did not say a word; she just stared at him in silence for a long time. He then turned from her, and stared again at the Distance Mountains before him. Then suddenly Dana impulsively turned and ran back to the mission house. Jamie watched her go, then with a sense of weakness, and defeat, stared back across the plains to the mountains again. Far away there were noises. He heard people stirring, the day was beginning, but for Jamie in some ways, it seemed like his was ending.

"Oh my God!" He cried out in emotional pain. "Please give me back my baby Dana! I know that I have sinned in turning my back on her twelve years ago! I know I do not deserve her! But Lord, remember, I have been forgiven by you through Christ's blood! Please remember me Lord! I really love her! I want to make up to her from now on! Please help me to do so. I promise to do my best, and be a good father to her from now on! I promise to, with your help, to never intentionally hurt her, or abandon her ever again!"

He stayed there praying to God until at last he felt God's peace in his heart. God gave him an inner feeling, through the Holy Spirit, that no matter what, that God does all things well. And that He will do the same thing for Jamie. Jamie felt that this part of his suffering was the type of experience that he needed to continue to do the work that God had laid out for him.

So what seemed like hours to him, Jamie then arosed, and looked off into the blue sky again. He felt within his self that all was going to be alright. No matter what Dana's decision would be that all was going to be alright. Once again he repeated to himself.

"I will not leave thee, nor forsake thee; I will be with you always, even unto the end of the world." With that thought that God was going to be with him always, regardless come what may, a special kind of

peace and assurance came and settled within him. He then turned and walked slowly back to the mission house.

"MEMORIES OF DANA'S SONG"
CHAPTER 9

The sun was so hot, and there did not seem to be any air any where! There just was simply no air to be found! Jamie had walked down to where they received their mail. Sure enough, as he expected, there was a letter from Nadine's sister Mulla! To him, this meant two things. One was that he would hear how the children where and also find out when they was coming home. Joy sprang up in his heart, because he had really missed them. It was true, that he was glad that God had worked it out so that they was away while this other situation took place. He was fumbling through the mail as he came upon the veranda. As he looked up he noticed Dana setting in the swing, making the swing go back and forth with one foot, while extending the other out in front of her.

He then noticed that she was singing a song that faintly sounded familiar to him. He knew that he had heard it before. In fact he had heard it quite a few times, but yet, he could not quite place just where! Her fancy dress was spread out around her in a lady like fashion. Her long blond curly hair was neatly combed up with a blue ribbon, which matched the blue in her dress, was pinned in her golden locks.

Jamie stopped, and stared at her as though he had just seen her for the first time as she was, a young lady of twelve years, who was blessed with all the good things that life had to offer. What a life she had! He thought. Immediately he thought of his little Marleiny, a child that was happy, and content to live the life of a Native American, and a missionary's child. Her long black hair that hung way straight down on her back, and the dark eyes that held so much earnestness, and understanding for her tender age. A little girl who truly was a laughing little dear! How could he ever ask these two to become sisters? With each of their back grounds, how could these two daughters of his ever get along? He wondered. How could this blond child of his ever be able to live in such a contrast? He thought this so much lately! Once again, he thought of him and Frankie of so long ago. THe difference in him and his brother, was the same as it is between Dana, and Marleiny. He kept remembering the feelings of trying to be as good, and loved by his parents, as probably Dana will likely feel about Marleiny. This made him wonder if he should even make Dana go through with that too. It was not that Dana was better then Marleiny, or the other way around, but it was just how that they had been brought up! So differently! Like a river flooding over a falls, it seemed so natural to him to let Dana go back home with Frankie, and Lorraine, and let them finish growing her up! It is so unfair to ask her to stay! He thought to himself. She was born to be fancy. To live as a princess! That is how Lorraine had brought her up. These thoughts came to him, as he looked at his lovely daughter, who was setting there so pretty. For the first time in the two weeks that they had been there, he finally saw these things so clearly. But he really did not like it. He knew right then and there that she could not live as Marleiny did.

Dana had not seen her father come upon the veranda, and she kept on swinging in the swing, and singing as though she was performing in front of some great audience. Jamie turned his thoughts for a minute, and listened to the words of her song.

"Tho' some times He leads thro' waters deep, trials fall across the way, tho' sometimes the path seems rough, and steep, I see His foot prints all the way!" She stopped singing the very minute that she noticed her father was listening to her. Jamie could not get over just how familiar that tune sounded to him. He commented to her concerning the song.

"Well what a pretty song!" He said, smiling. "Almost as pretty as the sweet young lady that is singing it! What is the title of it?"

"I must go!" She said, getting right up.

"Oh please do not! Please sing it again.' He pleaded, as he took a hold of her hand, in a jester to have her sit back down again.

"No!" She said, and yanks away from him, and moved fast toward the screen door. "Lorraine wants me to get cleaned up for dinner. I really have to go now!" She said over her shoulder, as she went into the house.

"See His foot prints all the way!" Jamie mumbled to himself. "See His foot prints all the way." He repeated the second time. This time he tried to let the words sink into his mind, along with trying to remember just where he had heard it before. Just why did it seem to hold such a special meaning in his mind? Then it seemed to him as though he could hear that song being sung by some one else, but who? He leaned back on the swing, and shut his eyes, and once again he tried his memory. He thought of his home back in Kentucky. He thought of the living room, and the fire place. Then the organ came up in his mind! He could see Merle setting at that organ, as many times he had come home unrepentantly, and found her at the organ. Yes, she would be singing that very song! Little did he pay any attention to what she was singing! For he had not cared! But he did hear it enough times that he recognized it!

"I will give you any thing for your thoughts right now." Frankie said, as he came out the door just then. He came over to where Jamie was still in deep thought about Merle, and the many things that went on while he made his home with her in Kentucky. Being surprised by his brother, he exclaimed.

"I was just thinking." Then they both laughed.

"I can see that you were! It sure must have been some thing deep! I will still give you any thing for your thoughts!"

"My thoughts are not worth anything! Jamie assured his brother.

"I am not so sure about that!" Frankie said, putting his hand on his brother's back." A man that talks to himself must have some thing worth while to talk about!"

"Well what are you, some sort of a philosopher, or something?" Jamie laughed. Then Jamie got a little more serious.

"Actually, I was just thinking about tomorrow. You are still leaving then aren't you?" Jamie continued

71

"What! Are you trying to get rid of me?" Frankie joked. "Yes man! I hate to think about it too. I kind of forgot until you reminded me. Yes, I do have to get back on the road again."

"Well, it was not that I was trying to get rid of you folks, because, as far as I am concerned, I would like you guys to stay on for as long as you wish too. But it is just that there are still so many unsettled issues yet." Jamie replied

Frankie looked at his brother. His thoughts then turned to the next day. The very day that they really had to leave for home. While he was thinking about it, Jamie broke into his thoughts.

"I was thinking about Dana. You guys had better take her back with you. She would be a lot more content with you, and Lorraine. She just does not seem to fit in here any where!" Jamie wiped his head with his sleeve. "What I am trying to say is that she does not belong here. Like you said, this is a crude and ugly part of the earth any ways! Besides she hates me! She will not take any time to say anything to me!"

"Well." Grinned Frankie; "I could have said that about you at one time too. I did not think that you belonged here either!"

"Yes, but that is different! I choose to come here. But she did not!"

"You may be wrong about that too!" Replied Frankie. Then jokingly he said.

"Do you think that I would give up a few weeks of vacation in my nice home, to come way out here in no man's land, if I did not have a good reason?" Then Frankie really did laugh then, when he saw the look on his brother's face as he said that.

"No, no, I am just kidding you! That is all I have heard for years! First Timmy, then Dana raving on about going to live with their father! Of course we had to find you first, and that took some time, seeing that you were so well hidden! If it had not been for that, we would have been here sooner! I must tell you, she has every thing all ready to ship to her after we get back." Frankie looked around him as though sizing up the place, then he kind of laughed to him self, as he then replied.

"What I have been wondering about since I got here is, where are you going to put all her things? This is sort of a small house!"

Jamie looked at his brother in surprise.

"Are you sure? I mean, really sure?"

"I could not be surer!"

"Oh, but there is things that has to get done yet! There are some things that I have got to say!" Exclaimed Jamie; "Things that has not been settled before...before she!" His words came tumbling out as though his emotions were pushing them out.

"Before I can even imagine her coming, and staying for good! There is Nadine! Then there is the other four, and the new baby!" Jamie rambled on.

"Oh! Hold it! Just hold it!" Frankie said, holding up his hands as though he could stop Jamie's words from coming at him in such a force.

"Oh, little brother, where do I start?" Jamie continued, paying no mind to what Frankie was saying now. "How can I tell her all about it?"

"First of all, you had better start by telling me. Just what about Nadine? And the other four and what ever you said? Oh the new baby!" Frankie said, trying to remember all the things that his brother named off.

"Well I just do not know where to start! But before I say anything other then what I already just said, let us take a little walk before dinner is ready, and I will try to tell you." Jamie said, as the two men went silently down the steps of the veranda and down the trodden pathway to the river. The same place where Jamie and Lorraine went that day that they spent together.

Dorothy LaRock Skinner

"TALKING THINGS OVER WITH FRANKIE" CHAPTER 10

"Well I do not know how to tell you. I have already told Lorraine. Did she tell you anything about Nadine and me?" Jamie questioned.

"No, she has not said anything about you and Nadine." Frankie answered;

"Well Nadine and I are married! But that is not all the story." Jamie looked at his brother as he spoke. He could see right from the start that Frankie was not about to believe his sincerity again, for the very moment he mentioned him and Nadine was married, he saw a look of unbelief, and pity come over his brother's face. Jamie wondered then if it would pay to continue with his story.

"Oh yes?" Grinned Frankie; "You want me to believe that you two are married?"

"Oh come on little brother, take me serious for once! I love that woman! And we really are married! I see no reason why we can not be!" Jamie said, defending himself. "I am more married to her, in a settling down way, then I have ever been to any one else! We are legally married by the law! I love her as much as I have ever loved any one! I am speaking the truth, and you just have to believe me!"

"So you really want me to believe that you married her, right? Why are you telling me now? Why not when we first came?" Frankie came back with such a force of words, that for a few minutes, Jamie felt that he had done something really wrong, by even saying that he was married to her.

"Tell me more!" Frankie urged. Jamie looked around to see if any one was around that might over hear them talking. Then he said.

"Well it is like this!" Jamie stopped right in the middle of what he was saying, for when he looked over at his brother, Frankie was shaking his head, as though he probably was going to hear a made up story from him.

"What?" Jamie asked, "You are not about to believe me any way, are you?"

"You know big brother, you are remarkable!" He said, ignoring what Jamie was saying, and already starting to form his own opinion.

"I often wondered just what kind of power you hold! Especially over women! Once you was back home having one affair after another, with heaven knows just who, and how many! Then you leave there, and get as far away from home as you can possibly get, and then you go looking for women again! Then there she is! You find this nice little lady, and wham! There is a new life, a new adventure, and a new affair all laid out for you! Go ahead; tell me about this new love affair! Tell me about this sweet little Indian woman that you have found! I can see that she is something special! She is nice, and she is sweet as can be! I found that out the day she went with us! She is very easy to deal with! Very easy going!" Frankie paused for a minute, as though he was carefully selecting out his next words to saw to his brother. Then he said;

"Isn't it funny?" Then he laughed, as to aggravate his brother. He then went on to say;

"I was with your wife, and you once again, were with mine! Tell me, did you have as much fun as I did?"

Jamie kept on walking, and did not interrupt him. But he thought to himself that he never really thought that his brother could be so cruel, with such sarcastic remarks. But he knew that his brother must be hurting too. They had not seen each other in twelve years, and Frankie must have been carrying all this hurt with him about Lorraine, and him, all that time. Yet, he really felt that his brother still loved him. Frankie went on talking, but Jamie's thoughts were too deep for his brother's insults to penetrate to his true feelings. Frankie continued to blast him with his nasty sarcastic words.

"Please excuse my expression, but how did you two make out that day you spent together? Did you both have fun? I never did get to find out just what you two did! Was the old flame still there? Did you both bring back some good old memories?" Frankie questioned, as he picked up a pebble, and tossed it off in to the far distance> There was silence for a few minutes, and Frankie continued to talk, and along throwing Jamie's past at him, with the same carefree force that he threw the pebbles.

"Did you do as she wanted you to do? You sure did have a chance to do a lot of special things, what ever to make you two happy! Actually I have not seen her so happy, well, let us say, for maybe in twelve years!" Suddenly Frankie realized that he had been rambling on for some time, and that his big brother had not said a word, or interrupted him at all.

"Sorry, big brother." He laughed. "My mind has just gone down hill, and been tired, and degraded through out the years.

When I was a kid, I could over look those types of things, but some times now, I have to let them all out. I have to see some one else hurt as much, or more then I am. I feel I can deal with things when I hurt some one near to me. Maybe it is my way of saying, wake up! Can't you see I am hurting? After all, who is the out law here? I am! It was me who has stolen her from you, I guess!"

By the time that Frankie had quit talking, they had reached the river. They both automatically picked up a handful of small pebbles, and took turns tossing them into the river, like two young brothers had done in the past. Both being lost in the moment. Then Jamie turns to his brother, and asked.

"Do you not see that I have changed?"

"Well yes you have changed some. Like maybe in a way that I can not quite put my finger on it, but you still like the women! I can see that for sure!"

"May I correct that statement "Jamie asked; "You mean my woman!"

"Can I make a little joke here?" Questioned Frankie; "They all seem to be your woman!" Frankie had thought that to be sort of funny, but his brother was being too serious to laugh.

77

Is that really true?" Inquired Jamie. "Is that how you really see me? Or is it the way you use to see me, and how you remember me to be? Why are you so critical of me? Who gives you the right to interpret my feelings? You know I do not really see you telling me this>"Jamie said, now looking straight at his brother now." When I think of Frankie, my brother, I think of a guy who really loved me, and who was always willing to do anything for me, even giving up the woman he loved! But when you moved in and took my wife as your wife, then jealousy moved in and took away that love! Jealousy always takes away love! Always! You know, when I hear you condemning me like this, all I can think of are that you are letting the devil use you to get to me! For it is he who is condemning me! It is the devil who knows whose side I am on now! I let him go! I no longer have to hear his crap any more! You, my brother are letting the devil use your mouth piece! You are literally letting the devil talk through you, to hurt me. Did you ever stop and think about that? In so doing, it hurts me more for you doing that, and then it does in what you are saying! Why do you let the devil do your talking for you? I ask this because I know deep down inside of you is a man who does not really approve of what is coming out of your mouth! You are just too intelligent to let him do your talking for you! Why do you not see this? Why don't you demand that old devil to just leave you alone? So you can say the things that you really feel? Give your self back that self respect that belongs to you! The one that you have worked so hard for! We are both grown men, let us start acting like that, and let us forgive, and forget those hard feelings, and grudges that keep us from being good brothers to each other. Once again, let me say. I do not want to take your wife, or life away from you! I have one of my own, and I am happy with my own! I do not need yours! So let us live, and let live." Like a little boy again, Frankie put his head down and sulked awhile. He knew Jamie was right, he was letting his feelings get out of hand! Jamie just sat there on the banks of the river, in silence. Then he spoke.

"Do you still want to hear my story?"

"Yes, sure go ahead big brother!" Frankie answered, but still was sulking.

"Will you try really hard to see it as it is, and stop thinking all bad things about me?"

"I will do my best to believe you! I am sorry for the way I have been acting, and thinking, that I want you to forgive me. And I will leave my judging for some one wiser, and less angered then I am, okay?" Frankie groaned.

"Thank you little brother, I appreciate that. Now what I want to tell you is as follows. After I left Kentucky behind, I became a missionary, then a pastor, and I came out here. It was here that I met Nadine. Her parents had died with a contagious disease that sweeps through this land. It took awhile to get acquainted, and it was well over a year before we decided that we really loved each other. We had worked together for the Lord, and we decided that we wanted to continue to do so for the rest of our lives. It was hard at first. I found it hard to understand her language, and her Native American ways, but she helped me. There were times that she did not understand me either, I did not blame her, and for it was times I just did not understand myself either! But we stuck together! Her constantly by my side! She never once demanded any exclamations for my actions. By the time the second year came around, we had a baby girl. We called her Marleiny. The next year Jeffery came along. Then the next two babies died within a year after they was born. We named the Rodney, and Paul. Their little graves are up on the hill just behind the little church building. These were sad years for us. It hurt so bad to let them die, and not be able to do anything for them! But I guess we had to expect things to happen like that. You know that there is so little to do with here at the mission. Sometimes things get pretty hard.

Then when Cory was born, and survived he sure cheered us up tremendously! We thought that our sadness was over. But it was not! After Cory, two more babies died before their first birthday! This really crushed me! I had then decided to leave the ministry, and take my family back home to Kentucky. But God in His great wisdom helped me realize that that was not the right thing to do. It simply was not the answer! I realized that Nadine, or my children would not be able to get along in our old world of the past, and I loved them very deeply by then! So I struggled within my self, and we struggled through them hard years too. Then God sent us Cherry, and Nadine said that she was a symbol of God's love to us, by her saying that, reminded me of what Merle had said about Dana, but I understood Nadine more then I did

Merle. Cherry is three now, and cute little tyke at that! In the spring we are to have another baby." Jamie concluded, shaking his head as those he could not believe it. By now Frankie had gotten over his sulking, and had settled in listening to the story with great interest.

"Go on, tell me more! It is quite interesting!" Remarked Frankie.

Jamie could not help but laugh at his brother's sudden interest, for Frankie was acting like he was starting to believe his brother!

"Well all there is to say now is, just as soon as this baby comes, and everything is all settled, and okay as far as we can see, then I am going to be sent to a mission in Australia."

"You what?" Frankie said in shock. "Whoa! You have got to be kidding me! Tell me that you are kidding me! He said.

"No! I am not kidding you, my little brother. We would have gone sooner, but they decided to wait probably until after we get settled in with the baby. But just maybe it was the Lord that intervened, I am sure He knew you would be coming and looking us up!" Jamie laughed." The Lord works in in mysterious ways you know!"

"Deep down in Frankie did not feel like laughing about his brother moving out of the country all that much! He had just found his brother, now he will lose him again! Maybe more! Maybe Dana! Maybe Timmy! He swallowed hard.

"But what about Dana? What about Timmy? Will they want to go there with you?" He questioned.

"I know that my family can take it no matter what! But I am a little concerned about Timmy, and Dana. I am still wondering if they will accept Nadine and the children yet!"

"Man alive brother!" Frankie exclaimed, throwing up his hands, in his 'I can not believe it!' way. "You sure love living on the edge don't you? You sure can make life complicated! I would dare say that you just might be throwing a cog in the works! You just might have created a new problem for your self!" He thought for a minute, and then asked. "Australia? Why in the world Australia? Will Dana want to go to Australia? He kept saying Australia, as though he was trying to get use to the idea of it! Now that is a tough one for sure!" He said quite serious.

"Brother..." he said; "Regardless what, or where you go, please promise me that you will not forsake us again. It took so long for me to get to know you when we was kids, and now that we have grown up, you left again. I can understand some of the logic why you left us, but it took a long; really long time this last time to find you! I am just asking you to promise me that you will not lose your self from us again. We need you, and I can see you need us too! It just seems to me…" Frankie choked up a bit, then went on, as he blinked the tears back that swelled up in his dark eyes. "That I will never see you again! Please tell me that I am wrong!" He turned away so that his brother could not see his weakness. Jamie, being a tender hearted man that he was any way, felt the pain that his brother was feeling, and he too blinked the tears back as he looked at his little brother.

"I promise you that we will see each other again. If some thing should happen, and God sees fit to take one of us before we get together again, I want to know now that you belong to the Lord, so that I am certain that we will meet again, up there!"

"But what are you saying?" Frankie questioned his brother.

"Well you have to be sure that you have invited your Saviour into your heart, and admit that you have sinned, and want to change>" Everyone has to do this in earnest sincerity. I did! You will have to. Do you feel you are ready for that?" I do not want you to do this just so we can be sure of meeting again, even if we die, but because of the fact that you know in your heart that you can not do anything alone. You need Jesus to be there for you, and to guide you out of your old life! In so doing, we will surely meet again! Maybe you have already done so, but if you haven't, then what better time then now to begin? I promise you that we will keep in touch, that will help, no matter where we are sent, and you little brother do the same! Someday, if God is willing, I will bring my family back home to Kentucky. I promise you that!"

On that note, the two brothers hugged as though to seal their promise. That night there was a meeting in the little church. Jamie's sermon was extra good. Many had come forth to the alter, and accepted the Lord. Frankie, Timmy, Lorramie, came forth and made their commitment . It warmed Jamie's heart to see his brother come forth to the alter. It was a load off his heart. IT made a happy time for Jamie and Nadine to see this. The only sad part yet was that Dana feelings was still in questioned. Jamie felt in his heart that he had to do some thing to change it, even though his time was running out.

"A WALK WITH DANA" CHAPTER 11

It was a nice night to walk, but it seemed hot to both Dana, and her dad. Father and daughter had some things to talk about, and the seriousness in her father's eyes when they left the church, made Dana a little fidgety. She kept curling her long curls around her fingers. After the meeting, he had asked her if she would wait, and walk home with him. She had felt that he owed her an explanation before she made a decision to stay on, or go back home with her uncle. He, on the other hand just wanted to be honest with her. Rather or not she was to stay, or go home. He felt that she should know about Nadine, and her half brothers and sisters here at the mission.

"First let us take a walk up to that little cemetery." He said, as he pointed up to the little hill behind the church. Dana sort of hesitated.

"I don't really like cemeteries>"She told him, as she wrinkled up her nose.

"Neither do I! But some times there is a quite peace that comes from the dead." He said gently. "You see I have a reason for taking you up there, because there is something up there I want you to see, before you go back to that big white church, and cemetery back in Kentucky. You do spend a lot of time in both places, don't you, when you are back there?"

"Yes, I guess I do!" She said with a sigh. "But how did you know what I do back home? Did Uncle Frankie or aunt Lorraine tell you?

Who told you? Besides, why do you call it home? Even though it might have been your home once, it is not any more!"

"Oh but it is my home in a way. Do you want to know why? Well it is because there are things, circumstances, and people, there that I love yet so that makes it my home does it not?" He asked.

"Well I guess!" She said, half agreeing with him. "But why did you give it all up for this place?"

"Well," He replied, using much thought as he spoke. "Because there are now things here that I love too."

"You mean a person! You mean Nadine!" She sarcastically remarked.

"Well yes, she is part of it>"He grinned.

"I thought so! I could tell by the way you kissed her tonight. You thought that no one was around!"

"But that was in the back room!" Jamie teased a little. "How did you see me do that?"

"I was being very impolite, I guess. But I came to talk to you, and I saw you and her kissing! So I decided not to bother you two!"

At this time Jamie was a little lost for words. He tried to think of the right way to tell her about Nadine, and him, but before he could find the right words, she spoke up again.

"You know I read a lot about you when you were a baseball player. You was really good at it wasn't you?" Before Jamie could answer her, she went on.

"I have heard about you and aunt Lorraine too. I have read all the newspaper clippings that my mom had saved, even those about you and other women! I guess you could say that I was being nosey, but I have read all your love letters that you wrote to mom too. I know she would want me to love you regardless! I know that mom loved you very much, and so I had to learn, because you were not around, to love you through her eyes! Mainly, because she did see something special in you. I thought that if she saw something good and special in you, that she would have wanted me to look for that in you too. But tell me, how can I love some one that I do not know, unless their goodness comes out to you? Like moms did? I must tell you, when I saw you there kissing Nadine, probably the same way you kissed my mom or even aunt Lorraine many of times, I just knew that you was not to mom, what she was to you! I figured that you were all that I had ever read about you!" Dana stopped to catch her breath, for she was pretty worked up from talking about this, but then she continued.

"You are not really true blue, and you being a preacher do not fool me. You being a preacher are a cover-up for who you really are! I have heard about people doing that sort of a thing! Even though you can get up in front of those people, and preach a tear jerking sermon, deep in your heart you still like to be you own selfish person! You like things to go your way all the time! Do you not?"

Jamie did not say anything, he just shook his head in dismay. He had been through this so much lately! He just let her talk. Deep down in his heart, he felt that a lot of it, at one time, was true, as to what she was saying. But three times now since his brother, and family had arrived, that he was reminded of his past sins, and was very tempted to retaliate! Three times the devil talked to him through some one that he loved, and held dear to his heart. He knew that even though he had sinned all these sins in his past, like she mentioned, he also knew that he had been forgiven by his heavenly Father! Because he had asked God to do so, and Jamie believed that God had forgiven him. To God, this past that she had talked about was all washed away. They were gone! He knew that he no longer had to feel guilty for them. He also knew that he did not have to suffer the second time for them either! So he just remained silent.

Finally they reached the top of the hill where the cemetery was located. There was a big bright Arizona moon, and it lite up the place well enough to read some of the names on the stones. They where mostly Indian names, and all sounding funny to Dana. Jamie took a hold of her hand, and led her to four small graves. Dana read the names. Rodney, Paul, Brook, and Jewel Mason. Her mouth flew opened in surprise, as she read the names! At first she felt speechless, and then she asked.

"You mean these…?" Her voice trailed off into silence.

"Yes!" Jamie said grimly. "Yes after all of this happened, I was ready to come home! But these are ours, Nadine and mine. I just could not leave her, or my God! As much as I wanted to go back home, I just could not leave here!"

"But how did they die?" She questioned. "Why they are all just babies, under the age of one! That is sad!"

"I know, I know!" He said, as he swallowed a hard lump that came in his throat, as all those memories came back to him." I know, and that is not all! We have four more that lived. You now have brothers and sisters Dana! Next spring we, meaning Nadine and I will have another new baby. Our biggest concern and prayers is that we will not have to leave it here!"

"But you and Nadine! How could you? I mean…!" She stopped in the middle of her sentence, and did not say any more just then. She just could not say what she did not want to believe. So her father finished it for her.

"Yes, we are married! And we love each other very much, and we love you too!" He said in hopes that she would see that they really did love her too.

"No! No! Do not ever say that she loves me!" She yelled back at her dad. "Do not even say that you love me or Tim when you know you do not! I know you do not! How dare you! You did not even love Timmy and me like you do like this new family of yours! You never were there for either Tim or I! Ever! We never knew what it felt like feeling a mother or a father's arms around us, and cuddle us! I admit that mom was not to blame, because I did not have her, but you, you just was too selfish to stay and care about me or Tim! You left us, with no thought as to what would happen to us! Do not try to tell me that you love us now! You failed my mother, and you failed me! You failed Timmy! Do not try to make me try to feel sorry for you, or you're other kids, because I will not feel sorry for any of yours! You deserve what you're getting; you turned your back on me on purpose! You knew just what you were doing, and you did not care!"

Jamie knew that what she was saying was painfully true. He felt as bad as he could for the things that he had done, and not done for his two wonderful children. They were not the blame that they were born! She started to turn and walk away from him, but he took a hold of her, and held her tightly in his strong arms. She tried to pull away, and resist, but he held her there, and she just let the sadness go. She cried uncontrollably for some time, while he held her there. While still hanging on to her he started talking;

"By tomorrow night your brothers and sisters will be coming home, and I would like it very much for you to give me another chance, and be there, so that you can meet them when they arrive. I would like it very much for them to meet their new brother and sister. Two of whom I feel is very special young people. I know for sure that they will love you. I know that they will just adore you, and love your long blond hair! But then again, seeing you are going back to Kentucky, you will probably never get the chance to know them, or even get a chance to meet them! You will never have the chance to know what it is like to have siblings, and a real family that is all yours!" He said. After a short time of thought he went on to say:

"You know, I feel that I knew your mom pretty well. I think I know just how she thought about why she had you. It was not only for me, but for you too! Like an extention of her. Know what I mean? I know that if your mom knew just how happy I am with this new kind of life, she would have wanted it this way. Cause she really did love me, like you said> I am pretty sure that if your mom was here right now, and you asked her what she would have you do, she would of said, stay with your dad! You belong to him! She would say that she had you purposely to be with me, because she knew that she could not be. I am sure of that! Don't you not think that Dana?" He whispered gently to her.

As Dana thought about what her father had said, it made her realize that with him was where she belonged. That is surely the way her mother would have wanted it! Besides, she needed her dad, even more then he needed her!

"Oh daddy, I do love you! I really feel that you are right concerning where mom would want me to be! I am really proud of you right now!" She said.

"I love you to sweet daughter of mine! And I am pretty proud of you and Timmy both! I am sorry that I was not there for either of you two, these last twelve years. I will try, but I know that I can not make it up to you two for all that lost time, but I promise I will not ever leave you, or turn my back on you again, unless it is in God's will that we part."

"I do want to stay; only I am not sure just how I feel about Nadine, and the others."

"Please just give it a try will you?" Jamie pleaded. "If you feel at anytime that you would rather go back home, then I am sure that your uncle Frankie will see to it that you get there! We will never know about each other, unless we have had the chance to get acquainted better, of course that will take some time."

"But daddy, there is so much unfinished business left in Kentucky for you! You left so many memories behind that you should take care of. If I stay here will you promise me that some day you will go back and tend to those things that you left behind? That is the only way you will be able to put them in the right prospective. Right now you have them all stored away in your mind! That is not good! You need that space for something else!" Jamie grinned at his wise young daughter, and said;

"Someday...someday, if and when I feel the need to return, then I will! But as yet, I still can not." He said sadly: "BUt I promise you I will,...Someday!"

"Oh thank you daddy! Thank you so much!" She said, as she squeezed him as hard as she could. "I love you daddy!"

"I love you too, dear daughter!"

"PROMISES MADE AND THE BIG DEPARTURE" CHAPTER 12

Nadine got up early, and went to her husband's favorite place of prayer first. She waited for him to come. Jamie was really happy to see her there waiting for him. He had missed her so much, and had longed to go get her and bring her back home with him. Now that he knew that things was going to be alright with Dana, he also knew that it would not be long before things would be back to a more normal routine. He had told Timmy about him, and Nadine and he took it really well. He had said that he was pleased, because he thought Nadine was a real nice person. He also said that he would do all he could to help make Dana happy in her new home. Jamie was very proud of his son.

Jamie took his wife in his arms, and kissed her tenderly. In his heart, he felt a joy of relief, and thankfulness, the sheer happiness, which one gets when they know that God has worked things out for them.

"She is going to stay!" He whispered to Nadine. "She is going to stay!"

"That is so great! My love, that is so great! I am so very happy for you now! It will be so nice to be a family again. It will be so nice for you to finally get all your children together." Nadine wondered to herself if it was going to be alright. She wondered if this was all of his family. She wondered if there just might be more surprises farther on down the

89

line. In her heart she felt very worried, but she did not let on for what she was alright with it all, and she tried to be excited for her husband. Excited like he was for it all turning out so well, according to his way of thinking.

"I guess so!" Jamie said, smiling at her. "I can say, I have missed my little family! I have missed you!" He said as he held her a little tighter.

After a few minutes together, they both headed back to the mission house. After they got there, they both started breakfast. He helped her in preparing it. They both wanted it to be a great meal, because it was his brother, and family's last meal together with them, before they had to leave for their home.

Everyone got up feeling extra rested, and happy. When every one got seated around the table, including Nadine, Jamie had them hold hands, making it a big family circle, and he said the blessings. He asked that God would keep them safe, and in His care until they all get to set down at a table together again

Regardless where that may be. Then like usual, he asked God to bless each one individually, and then he asked that He bless the food. It was a pleasant meal, and all too soon it came to an end.

Shortly, after the meal, Frankie started packing their things in the car, getting it ready to leave. Lorramie felt sad because she would be going back home without Timmy and Dana. They had been like siblings to her for so long. They promised not to forget each other, and write often. They all were kind of joking around just to take the pressure off. Then Frankie got serious.

"Now remember big brother, once again I am asking you that regardless what you do, please do not forsake us all again! It took so long for us to get to know where you where." He said in his deep voice, and sort of a scolding way, "Do not lose your self from us again! Do you hear me? We need you, and by all means you need us!"

"I promise that we will keep in touch. I will someday bring my family back home to Kentucky>"

Dana smiled at her dad, as he made that promise to his brother.

"You can bet that we all will be counting on that!" Frankie said. The two brothers hugged as though to seal their promise that they had made.

"All aboard! It is now time to go! The big Lincoln is leaving!" Frankie joked, as to take the pressure off the moment of them leaving. "Now that we have finally found you out, really try not being a stranger to us! If and when you get a furlough, come up to see us. Do not be afraid of what you will find back home, for I promise you that it is still very friendly. We all love you!" Frankie choked up again, and this time he could not say no more, so Lorraine said it for him.

"Yes, we will be expecting you to keep in touch with us. We all want to know just how things are going for you."

"Okay, one of us will write you often." Nadine said. Then Frankie walked over and hugged Timmy.

"I say, I am really going to miss you boy! By you leaving the house it will leave no male figure, except me to deal with these females! You let us know how you are doing, won't you?"

"I promise!" Timmy assured his uncle. Then Frankie turned and hugged Dana.

"Remember Danny, anytime! Anytime 1" He repeated. "That you want to come back home, and this goes for you too Timmy, just call me collect! You know the number! I will send out a posse, and have you back home within a twelve hour span! Maybe sooner! Try not to give your old dad or your lovely new mom any trouble, you hear? You know just how you were brought up, so keep that respect for your self, and those around you!"

"We promise! You have our word!" Timmy and Dana chorused.

"And mind your manners, you hear? I did not spend all those years training you to act the right way, for you two to go blow it when I turn my back, You hear?"

"We hear you, and we promise!" They chorused again. This time with some laughter from everyone.

"Come on honey," Lorraine said; "We have got to get going, we have a long way to travel. I am sure that the children will do alright!" She said, giving the children a big hug and a kiss good by.

Frankie and Lorraine exchanged best wishes with Jamie and Nadine, and soon they was into their car. All too soon they were driving down the road and out of sight. Frankie tooted the horn until they was out of sight.

They all got a laugh from Frankie's tooting, but to Jamie it was sad. He thought of the special people that had just left. His younger brother, and his ex-wife, and the sweet young lady Lorramie, and he wondered to himself if they would ever meet again. He felt in his heart that they would. He also felt some gratitude, and respect toward his brother, and Lorraine for taking such good care of his two children, and then graciously giving them back to him. He knew that it had to be hard for both Lorraine and Frankie to leave this precious cargo behind. He then vowed to him self that he would take really good care of them too!

As he thought about his brother and his family, he whispered;" May God bless these love ones of mine

"A RUN DOWN FROM THE PAST, AND INVATIONS OF INDIANS"
CHAPTER 13

That afternoon was hard for both Timmy, and Dana. Already they missed home, and their uncle's family life, that they had known. Jamie could tell that they were already feeling homesick, but he had no choice but to go to a church board meeting. On knowing that they was some what homesick already, and he would not be there right then for them, he asked Nadine if she could make them feel at home while he was out. She said that she would try.

"There is so very little one can do here at the mission for real fun, and entertainment." She said to the children, as she came out on the veranda where they both were setting.

"But if you like horse back riding, we can do that, if you wish."

They both acted surprised at her suggestion. Timmy really thought it would be fun, but Dana was not quite ready to give Nadine any standing room yet, so she did not want to do anything that she might suggest. Because of his feeling that he had to look out for Dana, and because he knew how Dana thought, he turned down Nadine's offer to go horse back riding. Then Nadine went in, and shortly, brought out

some ice lemon aide for them. Then she too sat down, and drank some.
Then she asked;

"Do you both have the same mother?" This was a question that had
been on her mind since they had arrived. Dana tossed her head, and
said nothing. So Timmy, after glancing over at Dana a minute, replied.

"No." He said politely. "Her mother's name was Merle, and mine,
well I do not know who my mother is."

"Oh, how sad!" Nadine said in a surprise, soft voice. "I just thought
that Lorraine was the mother to the both of you! Now I find out no?"

"No, but she is all we both have ever known." Replied Timmy.
Wishing to him self that Dana might pitch in here some where and
help him answer these questions of Nadine's. All this time Dana seemed
to be thinking about something. Her mind seemed to be churning her
thoughts, as Nadine went on.

"Your dad was married to Lorraine sometime? Am I correct?"

"Yes, but that was before he met Dana's mother Merle." He
answered.

"Merle? Was that before or after, Lorraine married Frankie?"
Then she added. "Your uncle Frankie is such a nice man, very good
looking too.'

Timmy was not so sure that he should be telling her all this. It really
was not his duty to tell it, he thought, but yet she keeps on asking, and
she really ought to know already! His dad should have told her by
now!

"Now let me get this straight." She continued. "First Lorraine?
Then Merle? But where do you fit into the picture?" She questioned,
pushing the subject further.

He sort of laughed, because he was getting a little nervous, and by
the way she talked did not help any! Then he thought he had better get
a little more serious, so he composed himself, and said;

"It must have been around the time he was with Lorraine, because
I am the same age as Lorramie is. But I really do not know who my
mother was, and how she fit into my father's life, but I have this feeling
that she did not mean that much to him, or else she would have a name!
And I would know, and hear more about her!"

Timmy's words struck a feeling within Dana. That was when she decided to let go the flood of information that she had been letting her mind churn up! She started by saying to Nadine.

"You do not have a clue about our dad and his past life do you?" Nadine shook her head no.

"But," She said, "I know that man that I am married to!"

"No you do not! You have no idea about his life before you! How can you live like that?" Questioned Dana. "No body will ever know him completely! No body knows all the crap he has passed on in his life time!" Came Dana's sarcastic remark. Nadine put her head down, and Timmy, in silent language scolded Dana. HE shook his head for her not to say any more. He thought that she should not stir up such a bees nest! Nadine did not see his expressions, and so she said;

"Go on and tell me what you know, you two." That was all that it took for Dana, ignoring Timmy's 'no we better not', she started to tell it as she knew it. As she had read, as she had heard, and as she witnessed.

"Well he was born in Brooklyn, N>Y>."

In one more attempt to get Dana to not tell what she knew, he warned his sister;

"No Dana! Stay out of it!" Timmy said, as he tried to be tough.

"Tim! She needs to know! It is obvious that dad is not going to tell her! They have been married for ten years, or more, and she still does not know! Someone has got to tell her!" Dana said with a stirred passion to tell it.

"Go on tell me." Nadine urged. "You say he was born in Brooklyn, N>Y>?"

"Oh man! Women, and their logical ways!" Timmy said, as he looked off across the sandy desert. He knew that there was no stopping either woman, from what they wanted to say, and hear. So he just stared off, and stayed silent, and let them go on with the whole thing!

"Yes," Dana nodded. "His father was in show business, and had an affair with some woman, who also was just starting into show business. When she found out that she was going to have his baby, she told him, but because he was already married to Frankie's mother, he denied this woman, and the baby, which was my dad!

95

Now this woman was hard up for money to provide for her self, decided that she could not keep her baby. So after she had him, she left him with a baby sitter, who was an older woman, and his mother took off and never came back for him! She just disappeared! Now the woman who was baby sitting took him as her own, and brought him up in the worst possible way, in the streets of Brooklyn.

When he became a teenager, he was pretty much out on his own. He liked baseball as a kid, and he created a powerful left hand pitch. Thus with this skill, he some how got into the baseball world. HE became a pitcher for the Brooklyn Dodgers, which later took him to California, when the dodgers moved to Los Angels. He was great, and became pretty famous, especially with the women. As you know, he was, and still is, pretty handsome!"

Nadine's eyes stared at Dana. She was not so sure if she should believe her, or not, because Dana seemed like the type who could make up stories for the fun of it, but Dana seemed to be on a roll, and very sincere about the way she was telling it, so Nadine kept on listening. Timmy too just sat there and listened. It was the first time that he had ever heard about who, and what his father was.

"When he became famous, and had lots of money, that is when he hired a private investigator to find his true father. Of course he found him in California, where the show business people live! When he found his father, he found a new family, which included Frankie, and his sister Bernadette."

Dana was telling all this as though she was reading it, as though she had memorized it, for she had! She went on with her story, while Timmy and Nadine both were taking it all in.

"After that he would go to California when ever he had time to do so. One time while on his way there, he met Lorraine. They fell in love, and were married. He arranged it so she could stay at his parent's place while he was away playing baseball. Of course his job took him away from home, and Lorraine a lot. It was when he was never around that Frankie fell in love with Lorraine. But she was so much in love with my father. It was a strange attachment."

Timmy looked over at Dana, as though he could not believe all that she was saying.

"What? Do you not believe me Tim?" She questioned. He just nodded yes.

"Every now and then she would find out that dad had been unfaithful to her. When he started seeing Timmy's mother, Lorraine found out about it, and left him. Frankie was there for her, and so she rebounded to him. The more dad fought the Frankie, and Lorraine thing, the closer they became. Dad hated the situation that he could not change He was like that! He begged her to come back to him, but she stayed with Frankie, and soon they were going to have Lorramie. Whether or not he knew the difference, dad was sure that Lorramie was his. It was his last connection he felt he had with Lorraine. About the time that Timmy was to be born, dad took Lorraine on a wild ride, bent on destruction for them both. They had an accident, and Lorraine ended up in the hospital all cut up and unconscious, and in labor. That was when Lorramie was born. Neither Lorraine, or Frankie knew anything about the baby, but was told that it had died from the results of the accident that Lorraine was in with dad. The trick was, that dad paid the hospital a big sum to lie to them. Timmy's mother took him home with her, and dad never let on that there was another child involved. Later she gave Tim back to dad for another large sum of money." When Dana said this, Timmy looked up at her in surprise.

"How do you know all this?" He asked her.

"Let me just say that I have had plenty time, and information on hand, to find out!" She said convincingly.

Nadine was worried that Jamie would get back and Dana would not be able to finish her story. So she urged Dana to go on with it.

"Please go on!" She said in a soft voice.

"Well, after dad paid the hospital to tell Lorraine and Frankie that their baby had died, then he took their baby home with him. He named her Lorramie after him, and Lorraine. When Lorraine left the hospital, she had to be in a wheel chair, because of the accident. It took her quite some time to be able to walk again. Of course she had no baby to take home with her either!" Dana replied.

"All this while, dad did not give up hope of the two getting back together again! He kept teasing, and using any way he knew how to get Lorraine back again! He kept this up until finally she did go back for awhile, but she was still married to Frankie. It was at this time, that

Lorramie got hurt, and needed a blood transfusion, and Lorraine was not able to give her any of hers, for some reason, and that was when the truth came out that dad's did not match, naturally! So in order to save her life, dad had to admit to Lorraine just what he had done in deceiving her! He had to admit that Lorramie was really Frankie's child! That Frankie was her real dad! So Frankie was contacted, told the truth, and he donated his blood, which saved Lorramie's life."

Timmy kept shaking his head in disbelief. He did not think that his dad was like that. But there was too many bits and pieces that fit into the puzzle too good to not be true! As for Nadine, she too found it very hard to believe that the Jamie she knows, could of possible been such a bad person. She and Timmy both urged Dana to continue.

"When Lorraine realized just how deceiving dad had been to her, she then packed up and taking Lorramie with her went back to Frankie. In feeling defeated, dad went back to California to try to get Lorraine to come back to him. On arriving there, he found out that his parents had rented his room to some young woman named Merle. Dad had always known that Steve and Rocky had a younger sister, but he had never met her up until that day." Dana took a deep breath, and then continued talking.

"Dad met my mom while walking to his parent's house. They talked, and then discovered that they both were heading in the same direction, for she was the one who was renting his room. Need I have to say, she became his next target? Yes, as he was so use to doing in persuading women, he set his sights on mom. He figured that it would really get to Lorraine, if she saw him with some one else! Now mom was brought up a Christian, and was a very spiritual person in all respects. But as for dad, that was something that he did not understand. He figured, I guess, that everybody had a breaking point, for he knew he did! So he tried to find moms. He kept teasing her to give in to him, and the more he teased, the more she resisted! Of course that added fire to his determination to break her. During all this time Lorraine did get jealous about his affair with mom. Now mom was not a strong person, and her health was not as strong as it should have been. Especially to deal with some one like my dad! She was considered pretty frail." Dana said, as she took a minute to think about her mother.

"Finally, she told him that she would marry him, but she wanted the wedding to take place back in her home town church, which was located in Woodgate Kentucky. She wanted to be married in the church that she was brought up in. She also told him that he had to give up his baseball. She wanted them to live in Woodgate. She told him that he had to be there with her, instead of all the traveling baseball players had to do. Now he was so determined to get what he wanted, that he would go to extremes to get it! Now I love my dad, but this is how he was!" Dana added.

"Well they bought a house in Kentucky, and they got married in that church. He got a job at the local high school as a coach. That job alone was a pretty good place to meet, and be with a lot of young girls! He never gave up anything! He cheated on her with who ever came along!" Dana said, with the air that she knew what she was talking about.

Nadine moved restlessly in her chair. She did not really want to believe what she was hearing, but some where deep inside, she sort of felt that it was pretty much the truth! But still she could not picture in her mind, the Jamie she knew, being as Dana had said.

"Are you sure what you are saying is true?" Nadine questioned.

"Yes, Dana, how are you sure what you are saying is all true?" Timmy spoke up.

"Well I am not forcing you to believe any thing! I am just telling you what I know! Whether you believe it or not will by your problem!" Dana replied.

"Is there more?" Questioned Nadine.

""Now if you want me to continue, I will!"

"Yes, go on." Nadine said;

"Well because of my mother's frail health, she was not surpose to have any children. He knew that too, but he did not seem to care, if it happened or not! So of course around the time that she found out that she was going to have me, she also found out that he was cheating on her too! He could not take the thought of a baby coming between them! He really did not want the responsibility that came with a family. It would just tie him down too much! Also tie mom down to some thing besides him! So with his nonchalance attitude he really made her suffer with his cheating, as though it was all her blame that she was going to have a baby! He even went back to playing baseball! Need I tell you, she died giving birth to me? I was born early, and was very small. I had to be put in an incubator for a few days, because my mom had a hard time having me! The day that I came home from the hostital, Uncle Steve brought me home. Dad took me from Steve's arms and held me a few minutes, and then he laid me down in my crib, and turned and walked out of our lives! No one ever saw him again, until now, when we came out here with Uncle Frankie.

Nadine looked as though she had a lot of mixed feelings. She looked straight into Dana's eyes, and tears ran right down her face. She could hardly talk, but she said to Dana.

"Thank you Dana for telling me all that. I have never been told that before, and no way to hear it. Jamie has never said these things to me."

"This will not make a difference between you and dad now will it?" Timmy asked, with some worry.

"No, my dear one, for you see, I have a different Jamie then the one that belonged to your mothers. My Jamie belongs to Jesus, and it makes me happy to know that your mother Merle did too. I can be thankful that she planted the first seed into his heart that made him the man that he has become today. I only regret that it could not have been different for your moms! I am sure they deserved better, then what they got. But it does make a big difference when Jesus is in your heart." Then she got real serious and said'.

"You young people should remember that." They both nodded in agreement. "I must go get us some dinner." She said, standing up, she smiled at them both, then turned and went into the house.

Jamie arrived back at the house shortly after that, and he found Timmy, and Dana in the kitchen helping Nadine preparing the meal. They all sat at the table, and ate. Jamie told them how the church board meeting went. When he asked them how their day went they all looked at each other, and then Nadine said;

"We all learned a lot today! It was a great day!"

After dinner was over, and the table was cleared, they all headed out side.

Jamie stood on the steps of the veranda, and looked off over the hot fields of the desert. He had no idea as to what went on while he was gone, but he felt a sense of serenity, as though he had been released from some heavy burden. He did not know why he felt this way, but he just did! After a time just staring out, he noticed a big old station wagon coming down the road. Its tirers were kicking up dust behind it as it traveled. He could tell that it was Nadine's sister Mulla's station wagon. Now Jamie was so pleased because he knew that she had precious cargo, his children! For a few minutes he completely forgot that there was any one else around, especially Timmy and Dana! No sooner had the station wagon pulled up to a stop, when the kids started hopping out of it! So glad to be home, and see ma and dad again, they barely waited! Jamie walked fast down the drivway to greet them. Picking them up and hugging each one. Everyone seemed to be talking all at once! They had so much to tell! Jamie was laughing at the children's excitement. Nadine came running out of the house, and ran down to where they were. She was so happy to have her world back together again! All the things that she heard from Dana had left her for this moment. A short time, Mulla took off, and waving to her sister.

Timmy and Dana stood by watching in silence. Timmy was remembering his dad back in the old days, and how he was now, this was the first time that he had ever saw his father as a real man. He could not help from laughing, as he saw his dad making the traditional Indian welcome signs to each child. He knew that his father had good relationships with these kids. Then thoughts of today came back to him, and he could not help but to feel saddness for Dana and him self, for he knew that they had lost out on having their dad be a real dad as he was to these children. Sadder yet, they even missed out on having their mother! Then the manly instinct that was taught to him by his uncle Frankie over took him, and he straightens his shoulders, and stood stately tall within himself. He knew that he had to do this for Dana's sake. He had to protect her from any hurt that could come to her! He then glanced down at his sister, and knew that he had been gifted to have such a pretty, sweet sister. He could see a jealous disapproval look on her face. He then slides his arm around her waist, and gave her a reassuring hug! He loved her so much, and cherished her within his heart, and he wanted her to get what she could get from their dad, while she was still young enough to do it.

"It seems good to see our dad be so happy!" He said

"Oh yes!" She snapped. "I surpose that it is the first time huh?" She turned in a haste to go in side, but Timmy sort of held on to her. He made her stay.

"Let us be a sport>"HE whispered. "Let us go greet those little Indians head on! We will either win the battle, or be taken hostage! Besides, we might just start liking those little rascals!" He then took her by the hand, and he led her off the veranda, and down to where his dad was talking to the children. As they approached, the children looked up in surprise. These were some body that they did not know. They wondered why they were there.

They all became silent, while Jamie told the names of each and every one. Then he explained that Timmy, and Dana was their brother and sister, and that they would be living with them. He asked them if they all would try to learn to love each other. He said that they all had a special place in his heart, and that he loved them all the same. Deep down in, it was hard for both Timmy, and Dana to really believe that he loved them, as much as he did these other kids, but either one said what they felt.

Marleiny was an easy going person, and because she was the oldest of these children, she sort of took on the job of looking out for them. She had a responsible way about her, so she right away felt the need to make these new family members feel welcome. She thought that Timmy was a real nice guy, and loved his looks, and his friendly attitude made her feel close to him right away. But she was not sure about Dana, other then the fact that she was very beautiful, and she loved the color of her long blond hair, to her it looked just like gold! She tried to assure them in her youthful way that she was glad that they had come to live with her family. As far as the other children were concern, they just let life take its course! They felt not much pressure from having them there.

After that day, time passed by quickly. There were so many chores around there that they all kept quite busy. Weeks buzzed by fast. With the church meetings, and all there was not a lot of time left for much of anything else. The family seemed to have knitted together quite well. There were some differences between Dana, and the other children, but Timmy, and Marleiny worked really hard to smooth off the rough edges. Marleiny looked out for her siblings and Timmy looked out for Dana. Marleiny tried to help by being kind to her blond haired sister and Timmy tried to bond with the little brother. Things had gone better then Jamie had hoped for, and he was very thankful to God for it.

Dorothy LaRock Skinner

"JAMIE RECALLS HIS SINS AND AWFUL SADNESS" CHAPTER 14

One day Timmy, who was always trying to be helpful, had offered to take Nadine, and the children into the big city of Tsaile, to do some shopping. Dana had wanted to stay home with her father, and get his dinner. Her reason for doing so was that she felt the need to talk about her mother. She needed him to tell her the way he saw it. She just wanted to see if what she had told Nadine and Timmy that one day, was all true. Actually she needed his version of it. She felt that his story should even out the balance, and set the records straight1 It seemed sort of lonely for just the two of them to sit down to eat alone, without the noise of the kids, but Dana welcomed the chance to be rid of her siblings, so just to have this special time with her father for awhile.

Setting there together seemed to be an uneasy task for the both of them. It was as though that one was bringing on a storm that the other one did not want to happen! That was how she felt! It seemed that any thing connecting Jamie to his past, still made him feel uneasy. Especially things concerning his life with Merle! After a long silence, he spoke.

"Say, Dana, could you tell me what the name of that song that you are always singing is? You seem to be humming it a lot to your self." By saying this, he knew that he was now opening up the things concerning Merle. Surprised that he should ask, she wanted to change the subject.

105

Yet, she still sat in silence. Jamie waited for a few minutes for her to answer him, then when she did not, he asked.

"Don't you wish to tell me?"

"Well!" She sighed. "I learned it back home. I ah, I use to sing it in the choir!" She replied, as though she just made the answer up on the spear of the moment. "I really did not go for singing in the choir, but aunt Lorraine and Uncle Frankie made me take voice lessons, and then they thought that I should sing in the church choir. You know, the church that mom use to go to! I had nothing better to do, so I DID!"

Jamie laughed. Then he said;

"You know it is funny just how some of those songs seemed to stick in one's mind>"

"Yes, I know what you mean! It is funny!" She laughed too. She then glanced at her father a minute. Then said;"Now do not get any ideas about me singing here at the mission church!"

"Oh no! But!" Jamie teased, as though that was the furthers from his mind. "I just thought that if you could tell me the words to the song, then I might possibly remember the tune, and as where I heard it from! I know it was not at that church that you first mentioned. I knew that it had to be from some place else! I just can not quite remember."

Surprised, she said quickly.

"Oh no! You would not know this song, because, I am sure that you did not go...!" She caught herself, and stopped talking for a few minutes, as she thought that she should not finish what she almost said.

Jamie knew what she was about to say though and that was that he had not been a good enough person at that time to even want to go to church at all! So he could not possibly know that song! She was right about that, but he did remember where he had heard it.

"You are right! I know you went to that big white church in Woodgate, didn't you?" He said.

She shook her head yes, then she went on to say, while trying to remember every detail

"It is a beautiful church inside, and..," Her voice trailed off in space, as she started to say more, but after a moment of thought, she waved her hand as though it would not make sense to talk about anything like that.

"Oh I might as well forget that! It is not anything that would probably interest you any way!" She said, as she pushed her chair back away from the table. She started to scrap the dishes. Jamie took a hold of her arm. Then replied;

"I have to tell you something about that church. That is if you would care to listen."

Then as they looked at each other straight into the eyes, it seemed like all of a sudden that the heat of the day was closing in around them, for Jamie was about to talk about something that had been long over due. It had been that something that Dana had waited to hear from her father alone! Dana had waited to hear from her father the things that seemed so important for her to hear and that were what life was while he was living with her mother.But she did not realize just how it would hurt her father to remember it. She felt that she wanted to hear it, but yet, she wanted to run away from it, or maybe just forget it! But looking right at her father now, she slowly sat back down in her chair, and listened.

"Well," He said, as though he was having some sort of a vision, or some sort of an out of the body experience all by himself. He started to talk;

"It all started so long ago! It was like a good dream that had turned nigh-marish!"

Dana could see the anguish, and the pain that her father had, just by remembering her mother's memories, and she impulsively blurted out.

"No daddy! You do not have to tell me! It is all in the past now," She exclaimed, as she remembered what Nadine had said about him being a different man now. "It is all in the past now, so let us just forget it! What do you say? Let us just forget it!" She kept repeating'

She put her hand on his arm, and to him, it felt so much like Merle's tiny hand.

"It is so much pain for you! I can tell!"

Jamie put his hand up as though he wanted her to stop talking, to stop telling him not to talk about it, and just listen to him. He stared at her and then replied.

"I guess I have to tell it! It has to be remembered! All these years I have been keeping it to myself, because I was afraid to tell it! I was afraid to hear it, or to even think it! But I realize now it was wrong to lock it all up! To keep it within me. I must share my memories of your mother with you, Dana! I now realize that I need to do this!" Jamie's eyes watered, and so did Dana's.

"This is where I have been unfair to you, I have failed you. I have kept each and every memory locked up so tight, and kept them to myself! I have never mentioned Merle to no one, not even Nadine!" Dana felt a little guilty about telling what she did to Timmy, and Nadine, but she did not let on that she had told them He continued talking.

"I blocked it all out! I have never tried to recall anything at all until you came back into my life. Perhaps that is why I never sent for you, or let any other person in my family know where I was! I was just too afraid of my thoughts, and my feelings. They just hurt too much! But now I know that I have to tell it all to you. For your sake as well as mine!" Jamie stopped for a minute, and took a deep breath.

"I met Merle in the spring of the year. May 18th to be exact!" He thought each word out as he spoke.

"It was muddie and slushie that day. It had rained, and stopped, but it was a damp chilly day. She was walking by her self. Neither of us knew at the time that we met, that we both were going to my parent's house! I had just arrived in Los Angels by plane, and no one was there to pick me up, so I started out walking. That was when I saw her! And naturally she was going in my direction! You see, I had been away playing baseball, and my step mother rented my room to Merle. I guess she did not think I would be back so soon, or else she just did not care! Anyway Merle needed a place to stay, and so that is how we met." Jamie replied.

"I had just gone through a rough time in my life, for I had just broken up with Lorraine. I should say, she had broken up with me! Because I probably would have never given up Lorraine, had it been my choice! You see I guess I could honestly say that Lorraine was always mine! I loved her like I never loved before or after her! But we had had some disagreements, and Frankie was there more then I was, so we broke up, and she went for Frankie. I guess he was more stable then I was, and she needed that. Well anyway, I had some time to kill, and with the thought in mind that soon Lorraine would wake up, and realize that it was me who she really loved. Then she would come back to me.

That is how I really thought. At least, that was what was on my mind at the time that I met Merle. Merle was a beautiful blond! Her eyes were your color, gray-blue. She was naïve in so many ways1 I admit I was attracted to her in so many ways!

Her spiritual ways was something that I did not understand! So she soon became a challenge to me, because of that! There was just that something about her that I could not quite figure out. She was so much different the Lorraine! I guess it was her sense to do the right thing, and live a clean and noble life, like her brother Steve! To put it plainly, she was a Christian! But I being the way I was at that time could not see that! Mainly because I was never taught about spiritual things, or about God, or His son Jesus! The only way I ever heard these names was in a cussing way. It just never entered my thoughts about such things being sacret! I probably did not even know what sacret meant then! At that time the things that was sacret to me sure was not God or anything! I was brought up to think that there is as much bad or more in people then there was good in them. And when I say good, well it still was not the good that Merle was! I had no idea just what good really meant. So I always focused on their bad. It is just as big a thrill for a sinner to bring another person down to their level, as it is for some Christians to raise another person up to their level." Jamie exclaimed.

"Anyway, I thought it would be fun to bring her down to my level. My way of life! Like I had Lorraine. I did not know until now just what made Merle keep her head through it all! As I think about it now, if she was into my Christian life, she might still be here with me! But that is just 'wishful thinking', and I do not like doing that. I know too late, just what she was all about! It was because she had Jesus for her Friend! And even though I did not realize it, it was this that appealed to me. I surpose that the Holy Spirit was trying to speak to me then, but I was just too far into sin to hear it while she was alive! And I was enjoying it too much to try to figure her out. The Bible says;"By beholding, one becomes changed!" Well I guess it is too late for your mother to know about how I have changed through her small life span here on this earth! It took a tragedy to change me, but it worked! The devil sure had done a job on me! He is still trying! Then I did not want to know her Jesus! At the time I could not see, or feel that power that it would take to change me!" Jamie said.

Dana listened with great sorrow, and sometimes pity for her father. She had longed for her father to tell his side of the story about her mother. She had wondered just what it would be, by seeing it through her father's eyes. So she said not a word, but listened while he went on and told his side of the story.

"JAMIE'S VERSION"
CHAPTER 15

"I was born in Brooklyn, and brought up in a slummy area there. A person does not have much of a chance to meet Jesus there. If one did meet Him there it is a good chance of them not really getting to know Him very well. Look, I lived right with a Christian, your mother, but I did not see Him, because I had no way of knowing, who or what I should look for! There is just too much against a person knowing, when all they see, and hear is taking the Lord's name in vain! Along with hating, and fighting tend the things that go with just surviving!

I did not know my parents! My father was not married to my mother, because he was already married to someone else! I was a so called mistake, through an illicit affair. My parents were in show business. They where dancers. When my mother met my father she was just starting out, where he had been in it longer.

When he found out that she was going to have me, he just plain took off, and left her! She had no way of knowing, and no money to find him!

After I was born, she left me with a so called babysitter, which could have been my grandmother, or aunt, but my mom left and never came back! To this day, I have no clue as to who she was, or what happened to her. I was never told. I never knew her name, not even her first name! She could be walking down the street next to me and I would not know! If she is no longer living, then I have no grave site to find her!" Jamie said, resigning to the fact that that is just how it will always be! He paused a few minutes, which to Dana felt like a life time, and then he went on with his story.

"I was brought up by this kindly lady, who had a lot of problems of her own. She was sort of sickly. The way I was brought up was not the ideal way! I learned a lot of filth, both in my home, and out on the streets, you probably know what I mean. I was brought up where anything goes!" Jamie shook his head at the thought of it all! He, himself could hardly believe what all he remembered about those days!

"When I was sixteen, and pretty wise to the world around me, a real nice man, who I had made friends with, sort of took over the father figure in my life. I was pretty tough, and fought anyone who got into my way! But he was there for me, and helped me out of a lot of messes! He also got me interested in baseball. He gave me the incentive to become some body! Somebody important! He helped me get into baseball. Because of him, I worked really hard, and before long I was making the big times! Now the lady that brought me up, died suddenly with a heart attack, and I no longer had her. So after the money started coming in for me, I made a dedision, and that was to hunt down my real parents. I felt, like you Dana that they owed me an explanation for just up and leaving me! Of coursae I had no idea, for what both of my parents was still together. I did not know at the time, that he was married to someone else! So I hired a private detective to find that 'rat' that is what I called him. Well, like I told you, I never ever found a trace of my mother! But I did find him! With the thought in my mind that he owed me the right to belong to him for awhile, I all of a sudden showed up on his door step, of his big old mansion! Of course they never had ever thought about me before, and so I was quite the shock to them. Especially to his wife, my step mother! So I opened up Pandora's Box, with my arrival! But after awhile they settled down to the fact that I was going to be part of their lives regardless! While making it hard for them all that I could, in every way possible! There was no way that he would tell me anything at all about my real mother! SO I lived there when I was not on the road playing ball. But any way, regardless how hard it was for us all, I felt good to have found me a new family, the one that I felt that I deserved from the beginning!"

Dana was happy that she finally got her father to start talking about him. It seemed to her that now she could relate to him in one way or another. She listened as her father kept talking.

"You could say Dana, that I had a sickness. At least that is how I see it now. I allowed the devil to have full control of me, well almost full control! He dwelled in this body of mine for years! Never once fearing that he would have to leave because of me accepting Jesus! He was so much a part of my life, and make up, that I did not really think about the things that was good! Infact, I hardly knew what good was, let lone be it, or accept it! I guess I just felt it was impossible to change, like a lot of people do, and what made it worst, I did not even want to! I did not even try!" Jamie exclaimed in his own amazement, as he thought about it.

"Now Jesus came to me through your mother Merle, bless her faithfulness! But it was such a hard ground to till, and plant, my heart was, that it took too much out of your mother, and it took me too long to see just what she was trying to tell me! I lived too long the other way! I guess in a way, I liked it that way, because it gave my life a challenge! But you know deep down inside me there was something missing! A big fat hole or something! I felt it, but had no idea at that time just what it was, and how it could be filled! I really had no respect for my self at all! I had no boundaries at all! I crossed them all! I saw myself being untrue to Merle, and I knew it was hurting her badly, but yet I seemed to enjoy it all! I did not want to change! I guess some part of me was afraid to change!" Jamie felt the guilt of his ways, as he talked on.

"Finally, she could not resist me any more! She was such a weak frail type of person anyways< and my persistence was just too much for her! So she promised to marry me if I would leave baseball. What is a promise anyway? I thought. It is just words! Look at the promises Lorraine and I made, did they get kept? So I went ahead and promised, just to make her happy, but I never planned on keeping any promises! Baseball was my life! I worked hard to get into it! Why should I give it up? Does a farmer give up his occupation? Does anyone who is trained good to do anything give it up all because of words called 'promises'? I loved the fans! I love the publicity! I love the way women would chase after me, and fairly tear my shirt off! Sending me mail saying that if I did not go out with them that they would kill themselves! I admit that

I loved it! I was not about to give this all up for one person! I thought that if I agreed to quiting, then after we was married, she would see how important it was to me, then she would love me enough to let me continue, as long as I spent time with her! But it did not work that way! You see Dana, once the devil has you, he really can come up with so many things, and ways to destroy you. That is his goal; he does not really care at all what happens to you, just as long as he can still your soul! And he not only works to drag one person down., like the one third angels in heaven falling for his tricks, he knows that he is going to go down big time! He plans on taking as many with him as possible! You see, the devil delights to have one of his great workers like I was, to wear out the patience of one of God's precious souls, like your mother! So you see, light and darkness does not mix too well, and it can never be a perfect union, unless one can cast out the other! As strong as Merle tried to be, and I was not about to give in any, our love could never be perfect! It was very, very shakie!"

Dana was still listening; even though she was hearing things about her father and mother that she did not want to hear. Jamie paused for quit some time. He made designs with some water that had got spilt on the table, and then he continued, as his thoughts about Merle stirred his mind again.

"We bought the big house in Woodgate, Kentucky. I got a job as a gym teacher there in the high school." Dana smiled.

"I know." She added. "They have your picture hanging in the library. Of course they think you are dead though. I use to look at that picture, and proudly say, this is my dad!" Jamie smiled, and then continued talking.

"Well I should say that Jamie is dead! He died before he left Woodgate! About that big white church there, the first time that I ever saw the inside of that big beautiful church that you are always talking about, was the day Merle and I was married. She insisted on a church wedding, and of course it had to be in that church! I could have cared less, just as long as I got my own way by her marrying me! So I went along with her. I remember just how lovely she looked! She was a beautiful woman! Her gray-blue eyes fairly sparkled with love. At the time I thought it was all for me, but I found out later that it was for Jesus. True she loved me, but she loved Him more! As soon as I realized this, I got very jealous, another devil trait. Besides I did not know Jesus then and it seemed like some kind of a threat to me. After we had settled down, surpassingly to be a happy home, little things started creeping into our lives that made me restless, and bored. Possibily this would of happen because of me being who I was, but I blamed it all on her and her religion! I started finding fault about her always going to that church every Sunday. At least twice a week she would go in the evening, which was what she called prayer meetings, but I knew nothing about that so I thought she was going to see the preacher! I would pick, and nag at her about it, but she did not seem to be moved in her spirit, and she went anyway! With all this annoyance, and restlessness that I had, plus the urge to keep searching for something that could fill that hollow spot in my life, I would go to extremes to try and discourage her with every ounce of power I had, and in any way I knew how, which at times was not too nice!" Jamie said as he recalled Merle in his mind. Dana still set nervously, listening to all her father's words. She was not so sure if she sympathized with him, or not, because the man that was now talking, was like Nadine said, hardly the man that she was hearing about!

"You know?" Jamie continued. "She even went when she was about to have you! I use to laugh at her, and bother her about the preacher. I would tell her that I thought that she was in love with him! I accused her most of the time about him. I thought of all the things that I myself would have done, and then accuse her of the same things. To me at that time, it just seemed like logical behavior! But through it all, she just showed me loving kindness, and she sure was long suffering with my abuse! Besides it all, she had this very understandable joy, and peace, that I could not destroy in any way! God knows that she did not get anything real and positive thing from me! But yet she was so long suffering toward me regardless! And through all these things, and many, many more, she tried to show me what a true Christian was really surpose to be like. She tried to offer me a chance to know her Saviour, but at that time I was too absorbed in my own sinful world to even let any of her's in. I more or less just laughed at her so called silly little sentiments, of which that is how I labeled them, and I just wiped them right out of my mind!"

115

There was silence for a long time, as though they both were thinking about all this. AS they both thought that they would have liked to have made things different, but they realized that this was how it was! Things could not be different! No matter how hard they wished to change it, it would not change now! For Merle was gone, and twelve years had passed! It was all there in the past, like pictures hanging in the halls of their memories, they must stay the same! Then after the silence, Jamie spoke again.

"That song you sing Dana, it was not some thing that you learned at that church was it?" She shook her head no, and blushed from embarrassment, for she knew she had lied to her dad. She knew where it came from; she knew where she had learned it. She only brought it up to begin with because she knew it was her mother's favorit.

"I knew it was not." He replied. "Because I remember that song now. I can see your mother at the organ late at night, with just the light of the fireplace flickering, there she would be gently, and quietly singing that song. You see she would be waiting for me to come home from a high school basketball game, where I had to coach. Often times I would not come straight home from the games, I would hang around with the young girls!" Jamie stopped talking for a long time again. He got up, and walked back and forth, not saying anything. Dana looked up to see if that was all he was going to say.

Far away there was some dogs barking, and for a minute Dana's thoughts wandered to those dogs. She worried if maybe they were barking at some cat, or chipmunk, or any other helpless little animal. Then her thoughts left the dogs and came back into the room, and her father. She noticed that he was staring out the window. She got up, and started clearing the table again, still half wondering about the barking dogs, and if her father had said all that he was going to say, or wanted to say. But Jamie broke the silence again. Making her once again to forget the dogs, and the little animal. That she visioned getting chased, or hurt, in her mind.

"It was that song that...!" His voice cut short his words. He sat down again, and stared at the floor. It seemed so hard for him to say what his mind was recalling, what he wanted to say, for his memories of it all seemed too over whelming to him. Dana stopped clearing the table again, and looked at her father. Then she spoke up.

"Maybe you should not talk no more about my mother." Deep down inside her, she wished he would stop, for she feared what he was going to say, and what effect it would have on him. It seemed to her, that he was having a very hard time just thinking about it, let lone say it! Yet she wished she knew just what was so hard for him to say.

"Why don't you?" She started to subject, but Jamie cut her short.

"No! No, I want to, I must tell it to you!" The way that he said that was as though he was telling it to himself that he had to say it to himself! Dana felt hot again, and by some force within her, she looked around for a window to open, but then realized that that had already been done hours ago! She then relied nervously on curling one of her long blond ringlets around her finger, as her dad continued almost as though he was telling it more to himself, then to her for the first time.

"MERLE'S DEATH AND JAMIE'S GUILT" CHAPTER 16

"I was not home when it came for you to be born. It was another one of those nights that I just had to get out of the house! Merle was not feeling good most of the day, and I should have realized that she might need me. Before I left, she sort of pleaded with me not to go any where that night. I just did not stop and think it through. I knew very well that it was not time for you to be born yet, and so I figured that it was just another bad day that goes with things like that! I told her that I would be over at the gym, and I would not be gone that long. I told her if she needed me, to call her brother Steve, and he would surely track me down! I realize now just how selfish and stupid I was that night! And as the night wore on, I got stupider! For I left her without another thought, just like I had did all those other nights.

At the gym, I met up with a young teacher who had just started working there at the school. We went over to a local bar. We was not drinking any strong drinks, we was just talking over a coke. While there a little while, a state trooper came in. He went up to the bar, and talked a minute with the bar tender, then they both looked over my way. Then he came over to us, and asked if I was Jamie Mason. I was still dumb about the reason why he wanted to know, and said;

"Yes, but who wants to know besides you?" Ignoring my smart remark, he then asked;

"Do you have a wife named Merle Mason?'

"Yes I do! Did she send you here after me? Is she okay?" I replied, as it clicked in my mind just why he was here looking for me. I stood right up, and grabbed my jacket, and started to head for the door, still not realizing the seriousness of it all! I just thought she had sent out a posse to get me back home with her again.

"You are wanted right away at the hospital! It is very serious, and important!" He said with a deep voice. "Would you like me to drive you there?" He asked.

"Yes you can!" I said, with no hesitations, knowing quite well that he could drive me much faster, then I could ever at that moment. After we got into his car, he turned his siren on, that was when I knew that things were bad! Well regardless how fast he drove, when we got there, your mom was gone! I guess what really got to me was the way that I had left her earlier; I had no way to tell her that I was sorry for my actions! I guess when things like this hardly ever happens this bad, it is hard to believe it could ever happen! But things like this happen so fast that one hardly sees it coming! I guess what really got to me was that I never got to see, or talk to her again. The last words that I spoke to her was very selfish, and careless, as I was walking out the door, leaving her alone, earlier that evening. Especially when she did not want me to leave her, to begin with! That was something one will never be able to take back. It leaves a sense of not ever being forgiven!

Tears were rolling down Jamie's face, and he wiped them off, but more kept coming! Being taught in his boyhood days that a man should never cry, he tried to hold them back, but just could not!

"After that, and the days that followed, my life became nothing but a blur to me. I do not remember going home, and I do not remember just who came to the house, or what ever went on around me." There was a long pause, and Jamie swallowed hard, then he spoke softly.

"I have no idea who made her funeral plans! Probably your uncle Steve did. It was that song that your uncle Steve sang at her funeral! Him, and her had learned it in church school, when they was young like you." There was silence again for a few minutes. Dana was feeling some what the pain that her father had felt. Then with so much sorrow, and grief, he spoke again!

"THey just took my life away that day! I begged them to leave her alone, but they took her away from me! In that big white church they took her! I will always see her laying there in her casket! She was silenced forever! She was just so beautiful, just like you Dana! You look so much like her! Even with all my money, my charm, my anything, I could not keep her from dying! And I could not bring her back! If I could have, I would have! But if she had the choice, she probably would have not wanted to come back! She was gone, and she was silent! All the peace of heaven was her's!" Like a big dam breaking, all those memories that Jamie had thought was sealed within him for ever started to give way! Like a flooding river, over flowing its banks in the spring time, it all came flooding out! Once again he remembered Merle, and what she had meant to him, and that she was really gone! Even though he had repented many times over, he could not bring Merle back "Oh daddy!" Cried Dana, as big tears rolled down her pretty face too. "I can see now daddy! I can see many things that I could not see before!" She put her arms around his neck, for she was feeling so sorry, and responsible for the way that her father was feeling at that time. But Jamie, as the memories continued to flow from his mind, did not notice her sadness, but kept on talking.

"The funeral was really tourcher to me. I could not bear the thoughts of Merle being taken away from me, and put into a black, dark hole in the ground! Every one was right there to suport me, but I could not respond to any of them. Then the days that followed! After they took her and put her in the ground, I would feel as though she was still at the church, and so I would go there. At first I felt that there just might be a mistake, and if I went to the church, that she would be there! I felt that I just had to see her! I thought, perhaps, I could go with her, or that she would come back and get me! But of course she never did! I was really messed up! You see spirits like that is only the work of the devil, and the Bible says that the dead will not come back like that! It says that the dead does not have any thoughts, or memory, just sleeps until He comes for them in the last day. Yes Merle was in God's care, and God does not work like that, so naturally this about her coming back did not happen! After awhile, I felt a sense that God did this to me to teach me a lesson, not that I did not deserve it, but because of this feeling, I began to really hate God! I did not know Him, and I did not know where He dwelled, because of the feelings I had, I wanted Him to come to me, so that I could talk to Him, and tell Him just how unfair I thought He was for taking her away from me! I thought that once and for all I would settle what He had done to her! Oh how little my understanding was about God! I did not realize at that time that He did not do this to her! It was my own selfishness that made her die! He came to me, but not the way I thought he would!" Jamie kept right on with his story and Dana just sat there and listened.

"Then, as time went on, it came down to the fact that all I could do was set in front of the alter, and just watch the candles flicker, and think of Merle laying there lifeless in her casket. I just would set there and say to my self, it is my blame! I was to blame that she was gone from me! I was the reason that God had to take her from me! Then I got down and cried that if God would give her back to me, that I would never miss use her ever again! I felt at that time it was a good bargain! But God did not, because that also is not the way God works! But I have learned since then that He never does anything unless it is for our own good. Everything that happens to us is to help us to find, and work out our own salvation! It is to help us to find our place in God's heart! You know Dana, anything that He has to take away from us, He replaces it with something that will help us more, and in the long run, it will lead us to Him! Thus making it better for us then it was before! Even though you, yourself does not see the way, He is there and He will make it right! You know Dana, since then He has opened the windows of heaven, and poured me out so many blessings! Many, many blessings! He replaced that which I have lost! I knew that I had sinned, and sinned, and sin again! I felt that I was too wicked to ever be forgiven! Well at least that is how I thought! But God goes to the depth of our souls, and because He knows the end from the beginning, He knows how we are able to change, with His help. So He counts us worthy to be saved! Because He exchanged lives with me! He took my sin and claimed it as His, and gave me His most perfect life! He is so good!" Jamie stopped a minute then went on talking.

"You know Dana; He came right to me there in that big white church! At first, when I felt all that guilt, I asked that God would strick me down dead, because I felt I could no longer bear that load of sins that I had committed through out my life time. I begged Him to make me die too. I pleaded, please let me die! I waited, but I did not die. What I did not realize then at that time was that I did die! Not like Merle died, for she died in the body, but my old filthy character died at that time! While I was pleading to God to let me die, I suddenly felt an arm go around my shoulders; it was that same pastor that I use to pick on Merle about. He had been watching me from a distance, and had been praying for me, while I was struggling with my terrible guilt!"

"Jamie." He said softly. "You do not know God! You do not know just how much He really loves you! He cared enough so to let you pass through all this pain, because He wanted you close to Him! He wanted you to see Him as He is, a God of love, kindness, and peace! That is something you have never really known! He did not take Merle away from you to make you suffer, for He did not want you to suffer at all! You choose it all on your own! You choose it a long time ago, way back in Brooklyn! He gave you so many chances to come to Him. Even now He is still standing by to give you just what He has wanted to give you all along! He really wants you to be happy. He wants you to be happier then you even can imagine! Especially right now! Now I think you are ready for it too. Remember there is Grace for even you! You know, He is a forgiving God! He is not willing that any one shall be lost, not even you! His salvation is free! It always has been! All that He asked, "He continued that man of God "Is that you acknowledge your state of being a great sinner, in which you have already done, and then be sorry enough to repent of your evil ways! And Jamie, He will walk beside you, and He will help you all the days of your life! He will forgive you, your sins, and cast them far from you!"

Tears came down both Dana and Jamie's cheeks. It seemed that at that moment they became closer. Dana understood her father better now, and she was glad the day that she was born, for she felt that she was born now to two special people, and for a very special reason. Even though her birth brought her mother"s death, it had brought her father life! Her mother had done her missionary work in witnessing to her father, and now it was finished well. Now her father was doing his missionary work too. Someday, she would be doing her share of missionary work! She loved him dearly, and was glad that she insisted

123

on coming to live with her father. Timmy was righ, she thought, her father is really a wonderful person to know! As these thoughts ran through her mind, Jamie kept on talking.

"That is just what I did too Dana! Right then, and there in that big white church, I realized just where, and how Merle gained the strength to live, and put up with me, and still stay the sweet person that she was!" Jamie concluded!

"But daddy!" Dana replied. "That look you have now daddy, you do not look like a man that was such a sinner, like you say you was! Tell me, does that come from Jesus too?"

"I am not sure exactly just what look you mean, but if you see anything that is good or great in me, then it most definitely has to come from me knowing Jesus, because I am nothing of my self!"

They both got up and started to clear the table fast, for they heard the car drive up the driveway out side, and that ment that their little talk was over, for the rest of the family had just arrived back from their shopping.

That evening while the children was being put to bed, along with Dana's help, for she seemed to have took a new interest in her little siblings. She especially took an interest in Marleiny. Jamie took a walk. He was thinking of how things was, and even though it was a hot night, Jamie shivered as though he had felt a sudden chill, for he was thinking of the things that he had told Dana that day. He realized just how long he had kept these things within him, and knowing that by doing so, he was still living with them! He had feared all these years to let it all come out, because he was not sure if he could face up to it all!

"Maybe by letting them out sooner," He said aloud; "I would have came a lot farther with You Lord!" Even though he had come a long ways already! He wondered if he had done wrong by digging up the past again, but of course that is something that he may never know the answer, or ever be sure of, except that Dana had a happier way about her; He thought of the children that God gave him in the place of the family that he never had! He thought of Dana, and Timmy, and how he loved them more then ever before, and even though they was different then his other children, difference was good! He thought of how much closer he had been to Jeffery, and then he had ever been to Timmy. He thought of the new baby that soon would be born to them, and automatically his mind visioned four little graves, and he then wondered if God would let them keep the new baby this time.

As he turned toward the house, he looked up into the sky, and watched a cloud cross over the big full Arizona moon, and he thought of the blue moon over Kentucky that he had saw so many nights, and he thought of Merle, and in his mind he visioned her laying peacefully in her dusty bed waiting for her Lord to return. Then he whispered;

"Sleep peacefully my love, and some day I will see you again>"

Then another cloud had passed over the Arizona moon, and then it seemed as though the moon got just a little bit brighter then usual, for Jamie had finally laid his darling Merle down to rest, and there did not seem to be any more clouds between him and heaven any more!

Dorothy LaRock Skinner

"HELL AND BRIMSTONE"
CHAPTER 17

Early **one morning, just before the sun had fully peeked over the eastern sky. Jamie was awakened by the sounds of some one pounding on his front door, and calling out.**

"Hey preacher, your church is burning! Your God finally poured down His hell and brimstone that you are always preaching about!"

As Jamie became fully awake, he jumped out of his bed, and ran to look out his bedroom window. The best that he could see, in the early morning light, was several men standing out in his front yard. He pulled on his pants, and rushed to the door. By the time he got to the door, and opened it, Timmy was right behind him. On opening the door, they saw a red glow toward the village, in the same direction that the church would be.

Glancing at the men, it was too dark yet to see their faces, but he knew that they had to be strangers! They were dressed in weird disguises. He could tell that the church was really burning, and he wanted to run, and help save it, but his feelings inside kept him from moving. HE knew that these men had started the fire, and he also knew that if he left his home, that his whole family would most likely be in more danger, then the church burning. He knew that they burnt the church, so to draw him away from his house! By the looks of these men, that they was strong men, and also dangerous! If they had been

someone that was for him, then only one would have delivered the message, while the others helped put out the fire.

"Well preacher, what are you waiting for? Are you not going to save your beloved church?" They laughed.

"It is in God's hands." Was Jamie's unmoved reply. They all laughed again.

"Well He had better get His big hands to work, or He will have to use His big hands to rebuild another church! Only we must remind you, that we will never let it happen, in this town again, but if it does it will be burned down again!!"

"God takes care of His own, and He has ways in which foolish men does not understand." Jamie said, still staying calm.

"What is it that you men want anyway? Why are you here?" He questioned.

"We heard that you have a pretty sexy girl here! We want the blond one! Send her out, and we will leave you a lone!"

Timmy's throat tightened, the fear of them taking Dana made shivers, and anger aroused within him. Jamie too feared, for the men could possibly have guns, so silently he was praying to God for help from these strangers. Strangely, he thought of all the strong men in the Bible, and he wished that one was there to help him out of this situation. He could fight pretty well in the past, but never really did it much. He was not a fighter!

"Did you hear us preacher? We want the blond girl! Send her out to us! Give her over to us now! If we can have her, then we will leave you alone! Then we will not bother you, and we will not burn any more of your churches!!" They shouted. Then one guy stepped up on the veranda steps. That was when, without any warning, Timmy pushed his way from out behind his father, and calmly walked straight and tall right up to the man on the step.

"Oh, a tough guy huh?" The man said; then he shouted out to the other men.

"He is just a kid!" Then they all laughed.

"I am not afraid of you." Said Timmy. Jamie then feared for Timmy's life. He thought Timmy could get hurt, and fear really gripped him when he saw all the other men gather around Timmy. The guy on the step gave Timmy a shove. On that move, before anyone had time to take a breath even, Timmy let out a blood curdling yell, and displayed Marshall Art like Jamie had never seen before! Right before Jamie's eyes, all the men fell like dominoes! It seemed to Jamie, that each man took his turn stepping up on the step, just to get karate by Timmy's powerful blows! It all happened so fast that the men barely acted like they knew what was happening to them! During this time Timmy had picked up the guys gun, and held it on them. He then demanded them to leave. They all very slowly got up, and walked back to their old truck. But before the driver took off, he shouted.

"You should not have done that smart ass!" He then spit on the ground. "Just be careful where you go, because, now we are going to be watching you, and you will pay big time!" He squealed his tires as he speeded off, kicking up dust behind him. Timmy came back up on the steps, still all hypered up from what he had just done. He was as angry at those hoodlums and trouble makers as he called them. Jamie was spell bound, and speechless. He hugged Timmy, and a few minutes before he even spoke.

"So!" Timmy said, "What do we do about the church that is burning?"

"Well, I do not know what to do!" Jamie replied, still amazed at what Timmy had just done.

"We can not leave the women folks here alone now, while we go help, can we? By the way, where did you learn to do that, my Samson of modern times?" Jamie inquired.

"Uncle Frankie. He made us all three kids get our black belt in Marshall Arts. I am glad he did! It sure came in handy sometimes!" Timmy said; "It sure helped get rid of those guys! I was a little nervous at first, but some thing strong took over in side of me when I thought that they might hurt Dana!"

"You mean Lorramie, and Dana both learned how to do that?" Questioned Jamie.

"Yes, we all did! Even though the girls did not want to learn it, Uncle Frankie made us!" Assured Timmy.

"Well isn't that something?" Jamie said amazed. "That sure makes me feel better about things! It appears that you all can take pretty good care of your selves huh? You acted pretty brave too!" Jamie said proudly.

"That is some of the things you learn, and that is not to let fear over take you. I thought for a minute it might though, but like I said something took over when I thought that they might hurt Dana. I sure love my sister! I would not want anything bad to happen to her! Not if I can help it!" Timmy said.

By this time, a messenger came running up the path.

"Pastor Mason! Pastor Mason! The church is burning! The church is burning!"

"GO!" Timmy said to his dad. "We can handle anything here! Okay?"

On that remark, Jamie went with the messenger back to the village. He did not really want to leave his family because of the strange men, but he felt that God was there watching out for them, through Timmy.

After Jamie left with the messenger, Timmy sat down on the porch steps, and in a low voice said to himself.

"Thank You God! Thank you Uncle Frankie too for making me learn what you made me learn. Bless my Uncle Frankie, will you God?" Then he set in vigilance, making sure no harm came to his father's house or family.

"JAMIE MEETS A STRANGER"
CHAPTER 18

By the time that Jamie reached the village, the church was almost burned to the ground. Every one was working hard to save what they could of their little church building. Jamie rushed over to one man that was standing by and asked.

"Does anyone know how the fire got started?"

"We do not know Pastor; it was surprising to us all!"

"Did anyone get hurt? Was they able to save anything!" Jamie's questions tumbled out.

"No, no one was hurt as we know of." Replied the man. "Just before it started to burn, we heard a lot of noise coming from the street. Some men, in an old pick-up, strangers they where, was hollering, and calling out bad names at you, they sounded like they was pretty drunk. We think maybe it was them that started the fire. What do you think?"

"Yes, it is a good chance that they did start it." Replied Jamie, as he remembered the scene back at his house.

"Some men came out to the mission home too."

The man looked surprised.

"What did they want? Did they hurt any of your family? NO?"

"No, no one was hurt. God sent Samson to help us out! God was with us!" Jamie said, after the man looked a little funny at him, when he said that about Samson.

"That is good Pastor! That is good! Nobody got hurt!" The man said shaking his head.

As Jamie watched the little church go up in flames, so many memories past through his mind. He thought of all the rebirths, the baptisms, the marriages, even his own marriage to Nadine, was right here in this little church! Now it was all gone! Now things would be harder for him, and his flock. And what made things worst, was the reason that some body felt that they had to burn it! He knew that it was the workers of the devil, for the devil had been on his back for a lot of ways, and reasons lately. That was the reason it happen! It was burn for hate, and spite. The devil was trying to give him as many blows as he could! Now it involved his sweet fair haired daughter! At that moment he felt that he could not stand much more of this retaliation, and he buried his face in his hands and cried! He had done a lot of crying lately. His sadness for the world, and the things that causes so much trouble, and pain, he cried for that. The sorrow that tries to hinder God's work, it was just so over whelming!

"Are you alright Pastor?" Came a deep voice above him.

"Yes, yes I am alright." He assured the young man who had just walked up near by. "God will turn this into something good! I am sure!" The young man replied.

"Yes He will son." Agreed Jamie, as he looked up at the young man. He then realized that he had never seen him around here before.

"You are not from around here are you? I do not remember of ever seeing you here before.

"Well I am just in from Texas. I am here on business." He said grinning.

"Oh." Jamie said, thinking to himself that how very seldom does this place gets people from out of town. "Where are you staying?"

"I don't really know yet. This is such a small town; there is not much of a choice. I do not suppose you know where I can lodge, do you? I could always sleep in my pick-up; I have a few times before.

"You are right, there are not many places, like you said, but you could lodge at my place." Jamie answered, without giving any thoughts of who this stranger was. It was then that he thought about the threat that the strange men had given back at the house, and he wondered if he offered to quickly, to let this stranger come in to his home. "By the way," Jamie continued. "How would you know that I was the Pastor, if you are new here? The young man laughed a hardy laugh, and said.

"Well my daddy always told me that if a man does not do any smoking, cussing, and drinking, then he was a good man! I could tell by the looks of you that you do not do any of that!"

"Well let us say your daddy is a wise man, but that does not quite satisfy me much>"Jamie said seriously. Ignoring Jamie's serious tone, the young man said;

"Yes, my daddy is the three 'W's' laughed the young man. "He is wise, wild, and woolly!" Jamie could not help but grin a little bit at that remark, for this young man reminded him of someone he use to know, his friend Rocky!

"Well considering that white cowboy hat that you are wearing,' commented Jamie. "Does that mean that you are one of the good guys too?"

"Yes sir!" The young man said, as he adjusted his prize worthy Stetson hat. "That is exactly what it means!" Once again giving that hardy laugh. Then he held out his hand to shake.

"I guess that I should introduce myself. My name is Dayton Lange. My daddy owns a big spread out in Huston, and his name is Rocqueal Lange. That is Rocky for short, except he sure is not short!" Then he laughed again. "He sent me here looking for a man name Jamie Mason. You would not happen to know the guy, who I am looking for, would you? He said he was a preacher, and you look just like the man in the picture that I have been carrying round in my wallet, that is why I called you a pastor."

"Well you found me!" Jamie said; "So you must be one of Rocky and Bonnie's boys huh?"

"Yes sir! That is my momma and daddy's name! Now isn't that something? Me finding you so quick! It was easier then I thought it would be! Just wait until I tell my daddy how quick I found you!" Jamie grinned, but thought in his mind, yah, I can not wait either!

"Well seeing that you are Rocky's boy, I must insist on you coming home, and lodging at my place. Infact, you may stay as long as you wish."

"Well thank you Pastor Mason. You know my daddy said that you would take me in when I found you." Dayton replied;

"Oh I never could turn anyone away, especially Rocky's boy."

By then the church was pretty much burned down to the ground, and the only thing left now was smoke, rubble, and ashes.

"We might as well head on home now." Jamie told Dayton. "Maybe the women folks will have some breakfast started."

"Sounds good to me! Here hop in my old Ford pick-up, and I will drive you." Dayton said, as the two men climbed in to Dayton's truck and they headed back to the mission home. Breakfast was waiting for them. Timmy, and Dana both recognized Dayton, and they was real happy to see each other again.

"So," Dayton said, "If you were to build a new church building, just where you would build it?"

"Well," Jamie said grimly. "The cost of a new church building would be just a little too much for the folks around here! It would take us some time to simply come up with enough money just to start it."

"Well Pastor Mason." Dayton replied. "Just suppose that money was not the problem. I mean the money situation, just suppose you had the money, where would you build it?"

"I suppose probably on the same lot." Said Jamie.

"Well if it was built there would there be room enough to build a school there too?" Asked Dayton.

"Well no, but," Jamie was not sure of what Dayton was getting at. "Why do you ask?"

"Well a few weeks ago." Dayton went on to say, "Frankie and Lorraine stopped in at the ranch, and they said that they had been out to visit you. They mentioned that you needed some money for your mission work that you was doing. So my daddy told him that he would match what ever amount that Frankie could come up with. Well let me put it this way Pastor Mason, they came up with enough money to build the church, and a new mission school, that is if that is what you want to use it for!" Concluded Dayton.

"I sure hate to have them spend their money on my account." Jamie said;

"Oh, that is their intentions anyway! When Frankie saw what kind of work you where doing down here, he was so impressed! He came to the ranch, and also impressed my daddy. They both ended up anxious to give money toward your missionary work. As for my daddy, well he loves to spend money in some way or another! Either for a good cause, or for a big celebration bash! That is what he calls a good time. Besides the I>R<S. will get it if he does not donate it to some charitable cause!" Dayton went on. "Besides too, my daddy has been looking for you for some time now! He says that you are his best friend, and he wants to do something special for you, especially since he has not been able to for a long, long time! But Pastor Mason, the way I feel about it is that, my daddy does not do a lot of things that is for the good, and why when SomeOne bigger then you and I impresses my daddy to move in such a way, well best you let that happen, who knows it might be my daddy's only hope! Don't you think so?"

"Well if you put it that way>" Jamie said, a little touched by what Dayton said, "Who am I to stand in the way of the Holy Spirit? I shall not refuse it!" Jamie said in a humble way.

"I am glad." Dayton said; "That makes me and my daddy right down happy! I am sure if my daddy was here, we would still have to have that big celebration bash! Just because you said yes!!" Dayton's hardy laugh, made everybody laugh.

"I tell you what< I will get right on my phone to my daddy, and in no time flat we will have a new church, and a church school up!"

So after they had finished eating their breakfast, the women folks cleared up the table while Dayton and Timmy went into the nearest city to wire his dad.

Jamie got around and called a church board meeting. The church board was very surprised at the prospects of getting a new church, and a school too. They praised God for sending such a special gift to them, so quickly after losing their little house of worship.

Dorothy LaRock Skinner

"THE PROJECT IN PROGRESS" CHAPTER 19

It was just barely dawn on the third day, after Dayton called his father about the money, when a truck hauling a big bulldozer, and another one hauling a backhoe drove into the main street of the mission town. The signs on the trucks, and machinery read; "Lange, And Sons, Constructions." Jamie, Timmy, and Dayton was waiting near the building site, where the new church, and school were to be built.

Jamie watched as the two tall lanky men got out of each truck, all with smiles and laughing. The young men were all dressed in western wrangler jeans, with work type shirts. They were all wearing a western type of hats. Dayton was pleased as punch to see his that his brothers had arrived right in the time that he expected them too.

"All right!" He shouted; "Now we can get started!" He ran over to greet them. They stopped about half way, and let Dayton come to them. They talked a few minutes amongst them selves, making hand motions, about the building site, and all around. Then they came toward Timmy, and Jamie.

"Tim old buddy!" Austin said, as he recognized Timmy. "Nice to see you again."

"Same here!" Timmy said in a happy tone. Then they all said 'hi' to Timmy.

Dayton laughed and said; "Now we are in business!" Jamie stayed quiet and waited for the boys to greet each other, then he said:

"Now I know that you are all Rocky's boys, but I do not know what your names are."

"Oh, I am sorry, Pastor Mason, I should have introduced you all." Dayton said apologetically. "It just slipped my mind that you did not know all of us. So here goes, this is my brother Austin, my brother Buddy, my brother Dakota, and my brother Dallas. There they are in alphabetically order!" He laughed again, "That is how our parents use to call us to supper!" He said jokingly, then he got a little serious, and said, "These are the guys that is going to do your digging." He pointed to Austin, and Dallas. "They run the bulldozer, and the back hoe. The blue printers are these guys!" Pointing to Buddy, and Dakota. "And this boys, is the wonderful Pastor Mason that we are to do the work for."

"Seeing your dad is my very best friend, and like a brother to me, you young men can call me Uncle Jamie, or just Jamie, which ever you prefer." Jamie said, as he smiled at them.

"Will do!" Dayton said, as they all took turns shaking Jamie's hand and acting pleased to meet him.

"As you probably guessed, I am the business manager of this out fit>" Dayton told Jamie. "And so if these guys do not do their job right you can come to me about it. Also, you and your church board may want to work with these two." Pointing once again to Buddy, and Dakota. "To figure out just how you want the layout, before those two," Pointing to Austin, and Dallas, "Start to do anything>! However, I must warn you, if you take too long in deciding, you might lose the diggers point of attention! They grow weary fast!" Jamie taking him serious, shook his head in agreement, Then Dayton laughed, and said: "That later thing about losing their attention was my way of lightening things up! They stick to the job pretty good!" Jamie did lighten up a little from Dayton's remark, but he could tell why Frankie thought it was so funny to see so many sides of his friend Rocky, in his boys!

"Also, maybe you would want them to dig a hole and bury these old remains of your former church that burnt, while you are figuring the layout?"

"Sounds right, and logical to me!" Jamie agreed again. Jamie was amazed by the way, Rocky's sons automatically worked together, all attending to their own jobs. No disagreeing what so ever! Finally, he said;

"I can not get over all this! All you young men belong to Rocky, and Bonnie! "After he said this, he got to thinking just how strange that these guys show up right the same day that the church burns down! If he did not believe that it all was in God's plans by sending them at the right time, he could possibly believe that Rocky had this all planned from the beginning! Except the situation back at the house the morning it burned when those hoodlums showed up! That was real! Therefore, he then tried to put the blame on Rocky out of his mind.

"Yes sir! That is us!" Dakota said;

"Well how many are there of you?" Questioned Jamie;

"There are thirteen of us all together! The young ones are still at home back at the ranch. No girls! My daddy calls us the baker's dozen! Those of us that are here is the oldest of the clam."

"Our daddy told us to get on down here and help our Uncle Jamie out!" Austin said; then he got serious and asked.

"Are you really our uncle?"

"I guess I was when I was married to your Aunt Merle. Now I guess I am just a cousin of your mother's. However, feel free, as I said before to call me uncle if you wish, because your father, being my very best friend is as much a brother to me as any one could be! We have been through thick and thin together once, and I have a feeling that we will again in the near future."

"I guess we have to tell you this, you are still our daddy's 'next to skin', that is what our daddy told us to tell you! Of course, he was just joking around, but he did get serious for a few minutes to tell us that you are closer then his next of kin. Oh he is always telling us tales about you and his adventures." Then on the other hand, if you know our daddy, you will know what he is like, and how he fools around so much. Hardly ever serious! Just a few times he gets serious!" Replied Dakota.

"Sometimes it is hard to tell when he really is serious, or just bluffing us!" Dallas added.

"I am glad to hear about Rocky again. After all these years that I didn't get to see him! Maybe he is just what I need now days! I am glad that he never forgot me, but when I think about it, I realize that Rocky is not one to forget those he cares about. That pleases me a lot, and makes me happy! To know I still have a friend like your dad!" Jamie said.

As the days that followed past by, Jamie could hardly believe the progress that the Lange brothers made in putting up the new church, and school! In addition, to top it all off, was that things seemed to be going along fairly well at the mission home too. Even Dana started to care about Nadine, and the nearer came the time for Nadine to have her baby, the closer her and Dana seemed to be. Jamie figured that this was just what Dana needed a family and home that she could really feel she belonged to. In addition, her mind was not so constantly on her real mother. Keeping busy with the work helped that situation a lot. Timmy was involved with the Lange boys, and spent a lot of his time with them! Brothers that he needed, Jamie thought.

Even those strange men never came back. However, Jamie was feeling more secure then ever about that, for now he also had Rocky's big boys there to help if it were necessary!

To Jamie, things seemed to be going along too well, considering all the things that he had to go through, back when Frankie was out! To him it sort of felt like the calm before the storm. It is that gut feeling one gets when things go along too good for too long! He felt uneasy. He thought about Nadine having her baby, and worried that she might have trouble having it or something of a similar sort. He felt that there had to be another trial or two in the near future. He wondered if there was any more of his past sins that he had to face up to! He prayed long, and faithfully for the Lord to help him through what ever it was that he felt so unconfortable about. He felt that what ever the Bible said was true, and it clearly stated that your sins will find you out, and even though he had kept this one sin to himself, especially since he Lange brothers had arrived, he knew without a doubt, that the devil would some time soon, would suddenly rise it to the surface. He did not know just how, or when, but he knew that the devil would try to destroy him in some way! However, because he had asked God to forgive him long ago of his past sins, he kept this one to himself. He never uttered it aloud at all!

It was spring now, and Nadine was soon to have her baby. That too edged into Jamie's mind like a burning iron. He remembered all those little babies that lay upon the hill in their dusty beds. Jamie tried his best to put all this out of his mind, for he knew that if given any room, the devil would play games with one's mind. He knew that worry, and fears should not rule a true disciple of God.

He worked close to Dakota, and Buddy on the layout, and he could see the gentler ways of Buddy, compared to the rough and rowdy ways of Dakota. He admired Buddy, for he seemed to be perceptive, and in every way accurate in all the things, he worked on. He used this knowledge to work out every little detail to make the church, and church school buildings strong, sturdy, yet beautiful, and appealing! Jamie enjoyed these hours spent with Buddy.

Dakota, on the other hand, was like adding seasoning to an already perfect stew! That is how Jamie saw him! His wit, kept the job going with the air of lightness. He reminded Jamie of his friend Rocky, for Rocky could never really

Get right down serious; there always had to be something to make you laugh! Thinking about his friend, which he had done so often lately, made Jamie feel good to be close to Rocky through his son Dakota.

Dorothy LaRock Skinner

"A STORM BRINGS BAD LUCK"
CHAPTER 20

The morning started out as usual. Buddy, and Dakota were on the job early. Dayton, Austin, Dallas, and Timmy had gone into the big city to get some supplies, and wire Rocky on how things were going. After Jamie prepared his sermon for the week, he decided that maybe he would just take a walk over, and see just how the boys were coming. He could hardly wait for the job to be done, for his congregation had been meeting in different places, but when the weather was good enough, and not too hot, they met out doors, or under a tent. He had told Nadine just that morning that things sure had changed since Frankie, and Lorraine had made their visit. Some seemed like good changes, but some seemed to be confusing, and mixed up. She agreed with him, and they both agreed that they would be happier when everything is completed!

As Jamie stepped off the veranda steps, he noticed some dust devils twirling here and there by the wind. As he walked every once in a while sand would whip up, and hit against his face. Then the dust devils would stop spinning, and disappear as though they where playing a hide-go-seek game. He walked faster, letting the strong wind blow him along. When at last, he got to the building site, he noticed Buddy, and Dakota up on a scaffold filling in for their brothers, who by then was probably having a great time in the big city, and who had probably lost track of everything, including the time!

"How is it coming?" He called up to them.

"We are moving right along!" Buddy shouted back, as the wind, now blowing much harder, with a mighty force, grabbed his words, and took off with them!

"Everything is going together like a celebration, and Irish whiskey!" Called Dakota, doing a little jig, as he clowned around on the scaffold. His fooling around, made Jamie's stomach feel like it was filling up with butterflies! He looked down so he would not see Dakota being so careless on the scaffold.

"I am afraid that there is a storm coming!" Jamie yelled back, trying once again to get his voice heard above the wind. Then they heard thunder, and some lightning flashed in the distance, and big splats of rain started. Dakota pulled his big-rimmed hat down covering his forehead and most of his eyes! Which made Jamie think of Steve> Buddy paid no mind, and kept on working.

"You guys! You better come on down now!" Jamie warned.

With the next gust of grit-laden wind, blow up, and it sent Dakota's hat sailing away like a bird! Dakota's reactions to the flying hat, made Jamie once again, think of Rocky, and had to laugh!

"You guys had better give up until after the storm is over>"Warned Jamie for the second time." These Arizona storms come up quick, and leaves quick, but they can get nasty in between! I am heading back to the mission; I have to be sure everyone is going to be okay there! Just be careful, you know like I said, these storms can get pretty rough, and tough!"

"Yah? Well we are coming right down!" Dakota said; "We will see you back home shortly!"

As Jamie got part way home the storm swept rapidly forward, wind, rain, and the thunderheads! Dakota climbed down and he then tried to see if Buddy was coming. Buddy, on the other hand, started to come down too, but blinking several times, all he could see was rain, and dust beating against him, thus making it impossible for him to find his way anywhere! He did not think that the storm would come that fast! He stepped one-step backwards, as the strong wind pushed him, and he stepped right off the scaffold! He fell backwards to the ground below. He fell just a short distance from Dakota.

By this time, Jamie was well on his way home fighting against the elements of the storm. When he finally got home, he rounded up his family, and headed for the storm cave. A place that was built for this very reason. Because of the bad storms that they get in the dessert, they need to be in something more durable then the normal houses that they live in.

After he got his family, all settled in, he started to wonder just where Buddy, and Dakota were. He was sure that they would be right along, like they said, unless something happened to them. That terrible thing that he felt would happen did! After waiting a little longer, he could not stand to wait any longer! He knew something had happened! With these feelings inside him, he decided to go back to the building site, and check!

By this time, the storm had passed through, and subsided, so he headed back. By the time he reached his destiny, a messenger came running up to him.

"Pastor Mason.! Pastor Mason! The man fell off the scaffold! He was hurt badly! Gone to city hospital!" He said, flinging his hands and arms up in the air. On hearing this, Jamie ran over to one of the boy's pick-ups, as he climbed in, he said'

"Go back to the mission home, no, maybe to the storm cave, but either place and you tell my wife Nadine what happened! Tell them I have gone to the hospital to check! Tell them to stay put! I will get back to them as soon as I can! Okay?"

"Okay that I will do!" Called the messenger, as he then took off on a dead run to the mission.

Jamie pressed the gas pedal to the floor, and went as fast as he could to the hospital in the big city. He prayed all the way.

Dorothy LaRock Skinner

"BUDDY'S ACCIDENT, AND ROCKY ARRIVES" CHAPTER 21

When Jamie walked into the hospital emergency room, he saw Dakota staring out the window. Right away, Jamie knew that it was Buddy that had got hurt. As soon as Dakota saw Jamie, he came right over to him.

"It was Buddy!" He said; "He just fell right off the scaffold! I am not sure just how bad he is hurt, but I wired our daddy! I am sure they will be here as the news gets to them. They can take a private plane, and be here real quick!" Dakota talked fast, and in a nervous sort of way. HE kept walking back and forth across the tiled floor.

Jamie sat in silence, and prayed to himself. Each man was thinking his own thoughts about Buddy. Jamie wished to himself that he had not left them while he went home. Probably it would not have changed things that much, except that he would have been there, and might have been able to have given him a better chance to survive this accident.

Rocky's long lanky body appeared in the doorway. Bonnie was close behind him. At the sight of Rocky, his dear friend, Jamie realized just how much he had missed him. He got up off the chair, and went right over to Rocky, and the two men hugged, both choking up from seeing each other after such a long time.

"It is really nice seeing you again, my old buddy!" Rocky said; "It really has been too long. How is my boy doing?"

"We are not sure yet." Jamie replied. "They have not come out, and told us anything. They seem to be taking a long time in there!"

About that time, the door came open, and a doctor came out. He walked over to where they all stood.

"Mr. & Mrs Lange?"

"Yes, is my boy doing okay?" Questioned Rocky.

"Your boy is losing blood from an internal bleeding. We will have to operate on him very soon!" The doctor said, stressing the fact.

"Well, what are you waiting for? What is the hold up?" Rocky said in an agitated tone.

"He has to have this operation soon, but he has a rear blood type, and we do not have that kind on hand!" Exclaimed the doctor.

Rocky stepped up front of the doctor, and with an assured confidence said;

"My friend here, the reverend, so happens to have the same type of blood running through his veins, as my son does. Try his blood type, and do it fast!"

"Is this so?" Asked the doctor, as he turned to Jamie. Jamie looked first at Rocky, then Bonnie, in a surprised way. They both nodded in agreement. Then he humbly said;

"Well it is a good chance that I do!"

"Let us check! Come with me." Therefore, Jamie followed the doctor in the next room. On checking, they found out that it did match Buddy's, and so Jamie donated enough blood for Buddy's operation. Afterwards, Jamie came back to the waiting room where Bonnie, Rocky, and Dakota was waiting. Rocky was pacing across the tiled floor now, while Dakota sat next to his mother trying to comfort her.

"This is not the way I planned on seeing you after all this time." Rocky said.

"Yes, I know." Jamie agreed; "Rocky, I am sorry that this had to happen!" Jamie went on to say. "I sure would not ever have let this happen, had I had seen it coming!"

"Well friend, I know you well enough to know, that you would never hurt one of my own on purpose! Do not blame your self! Some things

148

have to be, and there is nothing in this world to do to stop them from happening! We just have to live, and let live! Don't we old buddy?"

After Rocky said that, they all remained fairly quiet only talking small talk between the minutes, and hours that passed by. Finally, the doctor appeared. Every body looked up at him.

"Well is he okay?" Questioned Rocky.

"Is he going to be alright?" Inquired Bonnie.

"Yes, we think he will be alright. The parents can go in shortly to see him. However, he is not fully awake yet, and needs all the rest he can get. So make it short. Warned the doctor.

Rocky and Bonnie wasted no time going in to see Buddy. Jamie and Dakota waited in the waiting room. After awhile Dakota said to Jamie.

"How was it that you and Buddy have the same blood type? Why didn't they try our daddy's blood first, before they asked you?"

"Maybe he knew more about my blood type then he knew about his own. Maybe he knew at some time or another that he and Buddy's blood did not match." Jamie said, trying to satisfy Dakota. It worked, for Dakota seemed satisfied with Jamie's answer, and he did not press the issue anymore. Jamie felt relieved that Dakota was satisfied.

Then Jamie sat down in a straight back chair. He leaned forward with his elbows resting on his knees, and he put his head down. Dakota thought that he might be praying so he did not say any more to him.

While setting there, Jamie's mind took a trip back into the past. In his mind's eye, he pictured himself when he first went out to California. He was in his late teens. Bonnie's father was brother to Jamie's stepmother. Frankie, and Bonnie was close cousins, and they spent a lot of time together. Therefore, that is how Jamie had first met Bonnie. Bonnie seemed to be stuck-up to Jamie, so they really did not hit it off together much. At the time, Bonnie was dating Rocky, and that is how he met Rocky, and became good friends. Rocky was such a likeable guy anyways! He seemed to latch on to Jamie, before Jamie ever thought about being friends with anyone! Including Rocky! Shortly after Jamie came to California, and met Rocky, Bonnie and Rocky became engaged. Because Bonnie was all for Rocky, and paid no attention to Jamie, Jamie had to prove that he could get her anyway! He was sure she would go for him at some point, as he had thought about Merle! This was the kind of person that he was in those days!

This one particular night, he knew that Bonnie was alone, and so he went over to her place. When she came to the door, he pretended that he was looking for Rocky.She told him that he was not there. It was then that he pushed his way past her tiny frame, and got in. Because she was no match for his strength, he took advantage of her, and when he made his advances on her, she was not strong enough to fight him off, so he raped her. When Jamie thought about that now, he became so terribly ashamed of what he did. He found it hard to believe he could have been such a creep! Shortly after that night, she and Rocky left town, and got married. Buddy was the results of that night! It was never said, or publicly made known just who Buddy's real father was. Rocky and Bonnie never ever mentioned it at all. Jamie was not really ever sure, except he assumed it, but today, Rocky might as well came right out and told him straight, for Rocky stated that he and Buddy had the same blood type! In addition, it appeared that he was named Buddy, because Jamie was Rocky's buddy, or best friend! This all added up, without Rocky ever saying! The incident between him and Bonnie was never ever mentioned either, as though it had never happened. Now the thought really got to Jamie. He got up from his chair, walked over, and looked out the window. The rain was still coming down, and the wind was still blowing hard. Jamie blinked his eyes to keep back some tears that wanted to come. He said to himself, "Thank you Rocky, and Bonnie, I owe you a lot!"

"Are you okay, Pastor Mason?" Dakota asked.

"Yes, yes I am alright." Jamie assured him.

About that time Rocky, and Bonnie came out to where they was waiting.

"Is he going to be alright?" Questioned Dakota.

"I believe so." Rocky said.

"We thought that you two would like to go in just a minute to see him, now that he is resting better." Said Bonnie.

"Yes, we sure would!" Replied Dakota.

"We are going to wait here until you come out, but take your time." Rocky told them. As they turned to go see Buddy, Rocky called after them.

"Oh, by the way preacher man, would you just kind of say some hail Marys for him while you are there?"

"Why most certainly! I planned too!" Jamie said softly. They walked very quietly into Buddy"s room. Buddy lay silently against the white sheets. Jamie stood at the head of the bed looking down on his would-be-son. As far as he knew, Buddy was his first-born child. He was the one who should of beared his name. As far as Jamie knew, there was no one with his name to carry on. Buddy opened his eyes, and smiled.

"I scared you, didn't I Koty?" He mumbled.

"You sure did!" Dakota replied, "Man it sure was hard to finding you in that stupid old storm!"

Even though Buddy was still in a lot of pain, he managed to joke with his brother. Once again Jamie thought, one could sure tell that he grew up around Rocky.

"Pastor Mason?" Buddy said. "I hear we have the same blood running through our vains, now that you have donated me some."

"Yes, that is true." Jamie smiled.

"Does that meanthat I am going to be a good guy like you now?" Buddy said, in a weak voice, trying to joke while still in pain.

"Well let us put it this way, somebody has to be, I guess! Not that I am very good! I am just glad that I could be of some help to you!" Grinned Jamie.

"Seriously." Buddy went on. "I want to thank you for helping me when I needed it."

"Oh, I would not have it any other way! Now you know who to come to when you need blood again!" Jamie said, as he smiled down on his first-born. "I have one more thing to offer you." Added Jamie.

"What is that?" Buddy said as he looked up at Jamie.

"I would like to call on our heavenly Father, and our best blood giving friend Jesus, for your healing. Would you mind if I did that?"

"I would be honored." Whispered Buddy.

'Okay, Dakota you lay your hands on your brother, while I lay my hands on him too, and then I will pray."

At this request, both men laid their hands on Buddy, and then Jamie prayed for his total healing. Buddy felt a glow of peace fill his body, and he felt already that he was going to be okay. When Jamie was done praying, he said;

"We are going to leave you for now, so that you can rest. So just relax, and let the Lord do His work to heal your body. We will be back tomorrow.'

"That sounds like a good idea." Buddy whispered again, for he did feel tired, and wanted to go to sleep.

"Yes, little Bud, get better, okay?" Dakota whispered to his brother.

"You can not get a Lange man down for long>"Mumbled Buddy, as his pain killing shot took affect. Jamie and Dakota came back to the waiting room where Rocky and Bonnie was waiting. Rocky got up and walked over to Jamie.

"You know,' Rocky said. "I sure have missed you!" Once again, he hugged Jamie, and they patted each other on the back, as men will do. Jamie felt sadness to for all those wasted years.

"I am sorry that I took off and never got in touch with you in so long!" Jamie said, with tears in his eyes.

"OH that I will forgive!" Rocky said. "But what you did not know was, and that is, that I knew where you were all along!"

"Really?" Jamie said surprised. "Your not kidding me are you?"

"Nope! We knew! Didn't we Bonnie?" Bonnie shook her head, and agreed.

"We just sort of left you alone until you could heal from your grief." Bonnie said.

"Bonnie and I both felt that you needed a chance to make a change. Well you did! In addition, you did well, my friend! Of course you do know we kept our eyes on you, and we did say a few hail marys!" Rocky said, slapping his big hand on Jamie's back.'

"Well I feel bad that this had to happen to Buddy>"Jamie told them. "I feel sort of responsible."

"Well don't! You of all people should know that this is life, Jamie!" Bonnie consoled. "You should know if any of us do, that the devil is on our backs all the time! He never sleeps either! The day we are born, begins our day of sorrow>"

"I guess you are right." Agreed Jamie. "You are coming out to the house aren't you?"

After all this time that Jamie has been dreading for the day that Rocky would show up, now, in his heart, he really wanted his friends to come to his house!

"Well we thought we would stay in the city for the next day or two, to be sure that Buddy stays okay. However, we will be out before we go home. We need to celebrate you know!" Rocky said with a grin.

"Right.' Jamie said. There was that dreaded word again, Celebrate! HE expected this to happen! "Well then I will be running, so I will catch you later." He said, as he started to leave.

"Hey Jam!" Rocky said; Jamie turned and looked back at his friend. "Do not let the boogie man get yah!" THen Rocky laughed his hardy laugh.

"If he did, he would surely bring me back!" Came Jamie's reply. He turned again to leave.

"Hey Jam!" Rocky added; "I think he has already brought you back! You got to be too good for him to keep you!"

Dorothy LaRock Skinner

"THE NEW ARRIVAL"
CHAPTER 22

On his home, Jamie did a whole lot of thinking. Here all along, he thought no body knew where he was! But leave it to Rocky! He knew all along! Jamie thought of all the other things that Rocky had did in his behalf! He thought about, perhaps the church burning really was Rocky's way of helping him get a new one! It sounded just like some thing Rocky would do to make things look different then coming right out and asking him! It was so strange that Dayton was right there at the right time to cheer him up about the fire. The only thing that did not fit in was the strange men who came for Dana. That part was unexplainable! It does not seem like Rocky could of staged that, but then again, who knows?

He thought of how Rocky let him know, that he knew about him being Buddy's father, without coming right out and saying it! Or getting angry about it. It was kind of weird how Rocky had made a point to call him his "big buddy!" Things like this made him wonder about, just who had the best qualities for being a good Christian, himself, who claims to being one, or someone like Rocky, who makes no big issue about it, but does these good deeds every day, with no outward display? He could see well in his friend, which the world would consider foolishness! Even himself has thought Rocky was too wild, and crazy, but today he saw Rocky, his best friend in a different light! Not necessary wearing a robe of white, or a halo, or white hat even, but none the less, it made Jamie

155

realize that we all have our own shapes and forms, but still fit into one whole!

He then thought about Buddy again, and he compared him to Timmy. They both where a lot alike. He was proud of them both. He knew that he would never be able to know Buddy as his real son, like in the way that he had his other sons, because Buddy would always be Rocky's son! In fact, he thought, he would never ever be able to mention it to anyone, let lone Buddy. But there seems to be a price that goes along with every sin, and he is reaping some of the seeds sowed when he was young, and careless. Back then when he had no Christian ethics of any kind. At that time he just did not care, but now he hurts from his wild life!

He was glad that he could donate his blood to save his son! He was glad that he could be there for Buddy. Besides, he thought, there is more of my blood in him now! It was something only he could do! It was a silent way of being his real father! It was still another way that Rocky let him be a father to Buddy! But then another thought came to his mind, who was being the best father, the one who gave him his blood, or the one who cared enough to let him be born, and cared for him while he was growing up? The one that put his pride aside, and admitted that it was not his blood that ran through his son's veins! This thought made Jamie shiver a little. Rocky was the best father! In his own funny way, he was quite the father!

Tears rolled down his face, just like the rain rolled down the windshield. The wipers wiped the rain off the windshield faster then Jamie could wipe his tears away with his hand! He thought just how good life could have been had he not been bent on destroying everybody, and everything around him. He thought of the many children that God had given him through out his life time, and he wished that he had been different! He would like to see them all gathered around him, no telling how many faces there would be! He then pulled over to the side of the road and cried for all of them!

"I am so sorry my children! I was not there for most of you! If I could go back, I would try to make it all different for you all! I am so sorry my heavenly Father! Please forgive me! Please forgive me!"

The storm had made a big mess in the small village where the mission was located. There was debris all over the place! As he drove up to the mission home, he silently prayed that no harm had come to his family. He had left them in a storm cave when he left, but he could see that they was all back in the house again. He also noticed that the boys were back from the city, for their truck was parked in the drive way. As he walked into the house, he heard a guitar strumming, and Dana was singing. She sat in the rocker, holding something all wrapped up in a blanket. Dallas was the one playing the guitar. He sat on the floor, near her. The minute he came through the door, the singing stopped, and the younger kids came running to greet him.

"Daddy is home! Daddy is home! Yeah! Yeah! Guess what? Guess what?" They all chorused. "Look what Dana is holding!"

He walked over to Dana, and she opened the blanket for him to take a look.

"We have a little baby." Cherry told her father. "He is real tiny too!" She said, pinching her fingers together, to show her father just how tiny.

"Nadine had her baby" Dana said proudly. "Isn't it the cutest little baby boy you have ever seen?" She said, with the thrill of excitement in her voice.

Jamie nodded his head, as to agree, but asked, as he looked around the room.

"But where is Nadine?"

"Oh, she is resting." Dana replied. "The baby was born shortly after you left today. I helped birth him! Marleiny, and me, that is. We could not get anywhere to get a doctor, so we had no choice. Timmy said we could do it, so we did! Mom, I mean Nadine said to help her, that was all we did, was just doing as she told us too, and it turned out okay!"

"Is Nadine okay?" Jamie questioned, as he looked down on his new born son's precious little face.

"Oh, she is okay, just a little tired! We keep checking on her." Assured Marleiny to her father.

"How is Buddy?" Austin asked;

"He is going to be alright too. He had to have an operation, but came through it fairly well."

"I heard that you gave him some of your blood." Dayton said, as he came in from the kitchen where him, and Timmy were cooking up supper.

"Yes, and now that makes him my blood brother, and that means we both will be special to each other from now on, right?" Jamie said, looking at Jeffery, and winked.

"That is right dad!" Agreed Jeffery.

After talking to Austin, Jamie went in to see Nadine, to see if she really was okay. He then came back out, and took the baby out of Dana's arms, and held him close to him.

"So what shall we call this little guy?" He asked the kids.

"We took a vote on that before you came home." Said Marleiny.

"Yes and what did you all vote on?" Questioned Jamie.

"Well Timmy and Dana thought of the baby's American name, and Jeffery, Cory, and I thought of the baby's Native American name, and momma, and Cherry has already agreed." Replied Marleiny.

"Me too, I agreed daddy!" said little Cherry.

Jamie could not help but grin at Cherry, as he asked.

"So what did you all agree on, including Cherry?"

"Well, seeing that none of your children is named after you, we thought that maybe this might be the last chance to do just that!" Dana said seriously;

"So we want to call him Jamie Scott after our dad!"

The realization that she was probably right, for to the best of his knowledge, there was not any of his children named after him. The thought of a baby named after him, really brought joy in his heart, and also tears once again to his eyes! He snuggled the baby up to him, trying to hide his feelings. Then Marleiny added;

"And, his Native American name is "Gentle Lamb."

Jamie just nodded his head in agreement.

Timmy stuck his head in the living room, and said;

"I want to call you all out to the supper table! For supper is being served in the kitchen, so do not keep the cook, which is me, waiting! Get it while it is hot!"

Everybody laughed, and headed for the kitchen. Jamie took the baby in and laid him in his mother's arms, then he whispered to her;

"I love you both very, very much!"

Then Nadine whispered back;

"You have always made me happy. Now you make me happy again. You have given me a family! You have given me a big family! I know now that I belong some where! I belong to you, and your family!"

Jamie came out, and sat down at the table. Everybody was talking, and laughing, and even though he was awfully tired, and weary, he joined in on the laughter the best that he could.

It made him happy to see his family all getting along so well. The best reward a parent could ever have, and that is to have their own flesh in blood, get along, and love each other, regardless the difference they all had!

He could not help but think about how good a meal that the boys had prepared. HE also thought of his friend Rocky, and how he must feel having thirteen children, all boys setting around his table, but knowing Rocky, he probably made the best of it! Then he bowed his head and blessed the food, and thanked God for his family.

Dorothy LaRock Skinner

"THE AIR TRIP AND THE REDEDICATION" CHAPTER 23

Just when Jamie thought that he had heard, and seen it all, concerning his past life, some thing comes up! About a week had passed since Buddy went to the hospital. He had recovered very fast, and when he got released from the hospital, Rocky took him back to where he and Bonnie were staying in the big city. Jamie had wondered just why Rocky had not been around to see him. He had run into Rocky several times at the hospital, but so far, Rocky had not been out to see him at the mission home.

The church building was almost completed, and everything looked really good to Jamie. The new baby was coming along just fine too. Because he had bigger siblings to help Nadine care for him, he hardly had a chance to whimper with out someone picking him up! He was spoiled already, that was for sure! Thought Jamie. Well anyway, all these things going along so well, made Jamie feel uneasy, and wonder just what was brewing for the next big event to happen! He knew that he should not be thinking this way, and what ever God would see him through it, but yet this uneasy feeling still lurked in some corner of his mind,

One day, while Jamie was at the building site watching the boy's progress, Rocky showed up. HE got out of his car, and walked over to where Jamie was standing.

"Hi Jam! How's is it going?" He said in his usual layed back manner.

"Good! I am glad that you finally found out just where I live!" Jamie said, with a touch of aggravation in his voice. Rocky picked up right away on Jamie's mood, and came right back with his own comic remark.

"What? You have been thinking all this time that I did not know where you lived! Don't you know that the eyes of Texas are upon you?" Joked Rocky.

"Well it is just that I had not seen you around at all!" Said Jamie.

"Did you ever look behind you? You know I am on your trail! Yah, I know, you will just have to forgive me this time, Jam. Staying away was not intentionally, it just was not in my plans, but when Buddy got hurt, it made me get a little behind on my business, so I had to square that off. Say, how would you like to go for a ride in my airship, ales my private plane?" Rocky asked.

"When, and where?" Questioned Jamie;

"Well how about right now? I want to show you how she flies!" Rocky pointed up, and laughed.

"Well, I guess I could." Jamie replied, as he finally smiled back at his friend.

"Good! Now go tell your family that you and I are going to take an airplane ride, and also tell them not to worry about you, because you are going to be late, it might even take you into tomorrow, so not to worry, because you are going to be in good hands, your very best friend to be exact!" Half of the time Jamie could not tell if Rocky was kidding, or really meant what he says!

Jamie had no idea in what his friend had in mind, for knowing Rocky as he did, a lot of things could happen while they were gone! No telling where they might end up! But for some reason he wanted to go with him, probably because he had not seen him in so long, and had not had that much chance to visit good. He realized when he first saw him at the hospital, that he had really missed him. So Jamie went back to the house and told Nadine what he was going to do. She told him that he needed to spend some time with his friend, so go ahead.

"Remember, this is Rocky! No telling where he will take me! So do not worry. I will be okay! Keep Timmy around just incase you need anything, okay?" Jamie told her.

Rocky stayed at the building site, and waited for him to come back. Then when he got back, the two men drove to the airport, in the city, and then climbed into Rocky's private plane.

They chatted as they went. They had so much to catch up on. The plane was like an apartment. It had a living room with comfortable cushioned seats, and a small kitchen. Then there was a place for Rocky's drinks. Rocky asked Jamie if he would like a drink, as he poured himself out one. He told Jamie that it would just relax him. He told Jamie "You know I am never drunk, as long as I can hold on to one blade of grass, and not fall off the face of the earth! Jamie laughed but then said;

"No thanks."

"I can see that some things have not changed much. I never could get you to drink the good stuff!"

"I was crazy enough without it!" Replied Jamie.

"That was a good answer!" Joked Rocky again. "But how crazy could you have been, had you had drank some now and then? You will never know, that is for sure!"

They spent several hours in the air. More then Jamie could account for! They talked about the good old days, when they did crazy wild things together. They talked about how life had been to them since they have been apart. It was a nice pleasant time that he spent with his friend.

At last the air plane finally landed. When they walked out of the plane, Jamie could not believe his eyes! He could not believe where he was!

"Do you know Jam where you are?" Rocky questioned Jamie.

"I can not believe it! I am home! I am back in Kentucky, Rock! I am not sure if I want to do this!" He said, turning to Rocky.

"Yeah, you do. You really want to! I know you do! Besides it is all part of your healing." Rocky said;

"My healing? Are you sure I need this?" Jamie said nervously, wanting to go back into the plane again.

"Yeah, you do Jam! Yeah, you do! This is the last step, out side of the big celebration bash that we are going to have soon, this is the last part of your healing from your past." Rocky said, as he put his big arm over Jamie's shoulders, and sort of walked him down the steps of the plane.

"Are you some sort of an angel, or something?" Jamie said to Rocky. "Why do you feel that I need to come back here to be healed? Healed from what?"

"Well I am not an angel, or something! Angels does not drink whisky do they? But I am on a mission! My mission is to see that from now on there is no more 'spider webs' that you have stored there in your mind, to hurt you in the future. Today is reconciliation day! Today we reconcile to the past events! So let us go do what has to be done! You, and Steve, and me! Let's just do it!" Rocky said, in his own crude way.

"Well okay, but I still am not sure about this!" Jamie said reluctantly.

Down at the bottom of the plane steps, just a short distance, Steve was standing by his car waiting, when he saw Jamie, and Jamie saw him, they both walked fast toward each other. When they met, they both shook hands, and then hugged. Patting each other on the back. Tears of joy filled all three men's eyes. They was all laughing, and crying together.

"Jamie it is so good to see you!" Steve kept repeating...

"Yes it's been so long! Just too long! Hasn't it?" Jamie said;

"Too long brother! Too long!" Steve said'

The three men got into the waiting car, and headed for Jamie and Merle's house. Jamie seen places, and buildings, and landmarks, and so many things that was so familiar to him. They passed the big white church. Jamie stared at it as they rode by it. He swallowed hard, for it was there that he lost, and then gained his life. As they drove into the driveway of the old home stead, Jamie was so nervous that he was fairly shaking!

"I just can not do this!" He said.

"Yes you can!" Assured Rocky. Steve got out first, and went up to the door and unlocked it. Rocky stood by the car waiting for Jamie to get out. Jamie just sat there and was too choked up to move. Rocky reached in and took Jamie's arm.

"Come on Jam, you can do this! You just got to do this! I am sure it will help you face up to a lot of things!"

Jamie slowly got out of the car. IT was as though he was setting back and watching himself walk to the door. He saw himself as a young man, and going home to Merle, his wife. He followed Steve into the house. He looked around, and it was just like nothing had ever been moved out of its place. Nothing had changed! In a trance like way, he walked into the living room where Merle's organ was. He walked over and looked at the pictures that sat around.

Still in a trance like, he picked up Merle's picture, and stared at it so long. Tears rolled down his face as he touched his finger across her face. The glass felt cold. There was no warmth there except the love he had had for her once. He touched the keys on the organ, and he could almost hear it playing those familiar tunes. He could hear her voice loud and clear! HE walked from room to room, and then up the stairs he went to their bedroom.

Rocky and Steve just stood by in silence.

Into the bedroom he remembered all the love that him, and Merle had shared there. He picked up the pillow that was on her side of the bed, and he held it to his face. Although the scent of her perfume had long faded away, he could still remember the smell of it. He gently laid her pillow back down in its place, on the bed. Then he walked into the nursery, and there he recalled the day that he laid baby Dana in her crib. He then thought about his new baby he has now, and how much comfort he gets from just holding him, then he thought of how he had never gave baby Dana a chance to comfort him, like she was meant to do! It was then that he really cried hard, Rocky and Steve just remained still. After some time, he silently walked out of the room and closed the door, just as he had done twelve years ago. He gently and quietly closed the door to their bedroom too, and came back down the stairs again. He stood in the door way of the living room, and once again, in his mind, he heard Merle singing. He then turned and went back to the kitchen, and stared around remembering Merle getting his meals at the stove.

"I have to go now, Merle baby." He said softly. "But it was nice to be able to spend this special time with you again." He said, and then he turned and walked out the door.

Rocky and Steve looked at each other, in a sad way, and then they both followed Jamie out the door. Once they were back in the car again, they drove in silence over to the cementery. When they pulled up there and stopped, Jamie automatically got out. He walked over to Merle's grave, and read the writing on the stone.

Merle Marie Mason, born July 8, 1974, died May 18, 1992. Below it read; "Here sleeps the sweetest girl that has ever lived." Jamie then fell down on his knees, and cried again.

"I love you sweet Merle! I am so sorry! Someday, we are going to meet again, this I promise you!"

Rocky and Steve both waited for all that sadness to leave Jamie, and then they both helped him up, and led him back to the car. As they drove past the church, Jamie said;

"I would like to stop here a minute.'

"Are you sure Jam? Can you take any more?" Rocky asked.

"Yes, I am sure. Jamie assured them.

Steve turned the car around, and went back to the church. He parked the car, and Jamie got out.

"I can do this by myself." Jamie once again assured his friends.

So Steve and Rocky waited, standing out side by the car. Jamie walked up the steps and into the sanctuary, and down that long aisle. When he got up to the front of the church, he lite two candles, and then bowed at the alter.

"My dear Father in heaven,' He whispered; "Once I thought I was okay, and then You showed me that I was not! So I, in faith asked You to help me change, and I believed You did as I ask, for I felt okay, only in a different way then I did before, and what so ever things that were gained to me, those things I have counted as a loss for the sake of Christ, You Son. More then that< I count all things to be a loss in view of the surpressing value of knowing Christ Jesus my Lord. For His sake I have lost everything, and value it all as mere refuse, inorder to gain Christ and actually in union with Him. I say this not because I have already secured perfection, but I long to capture it. So I here by leave with You those things that are behind me, and I am reaching out for those things that are ahead of me, and seek to find that heavenly prize that God has called me in Jesus Christ. I now feel at peace with myself now. I have nothing to hide, or be ashamed of. I have loved Lorraine, I have loved Merle, and I have loved Nadine all at different times, in different ways, but all equeal ways. So Lord, please let this be a new ending, the ending of my wicked sinful past, and let this be a new beginning to for me. Please help me to change the things that has to be changed, and accept the things that I have no power over, and let me see and know the difference. I here by leave with You my past, please take care of it in the way that You see fit to, and go with me from this time forward, for my true love lies with You, and what You would have me do. I am asking You this in Thy precious Son's name, Jesus who holds all power! AMEN"

Jamie finished his prayer and got up, and slowly walked out of the church. When he saw Rocky, and Steve, he said.

"Well now I am ready to go, for now I realize that there is a time fore every thing, and my time for sadness, and weeping is over, Now is the time to laugh and be happy! A time for celebrating!" Jamie said;

"Now you are talking my kind of language friend!" Rocky said;

Then they all got back into the car, and drove to the airport. Just before they aboarded the plane, Steve said;

"It truly has been great seeing you again> I hope to see you again soon, and I hope it will be a happy occasion!" The two men hugged again, and Jamie said'

"Thank you steve. You and Rocky have sure been a great friend to me. I will never forget you. I will always remember you in my prayers!"

"Same here!" Steve said. "Will be out to see you some time soon!"

Jamie nodded his head in agreement, and then said;

"That I will hold you to it!"

Dorothy LaRock Skinner

"CELEBRATION TIME" CHAPTER 24

Rocky and Bonnie came to Jamie's house one night for supper. That was when Rocky informed Jamie that he had to go back to Texas, and straighten out some of his business affairs there. But, he warned his friend, that he would be back for a big celebration. Jamie cringed at the thought of Rocky's celebrations! He remembered full well just what all they consisted of! He use to put up with them because they were Rocky's ideas, and way of having fun! A lot of it he would just stay away from! But now days, he has a conscience that he has to deal with! He wondered just what his flock would think of him if he allowed a party, with drinking, and what else goes on with that type of thing! He did not want to hurt his friends, but he also did not want his flock to think he approved of that kind of a party either! He knew that Rocky was what the world would call an alcoholic, even though no one had ever came right out and said it. He knew him since he was a teenager, and he drank then, and he still drinks! He does not settle for the plain old beer, he has to go for the hard core whiskey! Still in all, he just could not tell Rocky that he did not want any alcohol around. He wished that Rocky would see that, but he knew that it was a slim chance of it! On the other hand, Rocky had been great! Why if he had not of pitched in, there would not have been any church, or school at all!

"How does a person handle things like that?" He asked Nadine.

"Well honey, the Lord loves Rocky as much as he does anyone else! He has already worked that out! It is not your problem! It does not reflect anything on you at all! Leave it to the Holy Spirit, my love! Leave it to the Holy Spirit! You must not judge, or hurt Rocky or you may never see him again! Besides, if you judge, you may never be able to lead him to his Saviour.' She said calmly.

"You are right again!" Jamie told her. "I will pray, and leave it in the Lord's hands. I know He will take care of His business!" So that is what he did. But he still wondered just how it was going to turn out!

It took three weeks from the time that Rocky, and Bonnie came to visit with them, that the church, and school building was completed. It was a long three weeks for Jamie! He looked forward to the completion of the church, and school, but deep inside, he dreaded the time of the celebration! He just could not fit Rocky into the picture at all! But he still believed that the Lord would work it out!

The celebration was all that he heard from the children. It seemed that that was all that they could think, or talk about. As much as he loved seeing his family, and old friends, it seemed that they just turned his world up side down! There were things that were going on that he would not have dreamed it could, or would ever happen to him, in his new life!

Jamie thought of how nice it would be if every body looked forward to the Lord's return, like they did for something like this celebration! He knew that as soon as Rocky returned that they would be dedicating the church, and school. He hoped that Rocky would not want to break a bottle of champagne to christen the new building> He could picture Rocky wanting to do just that! It sounded just like something he would try to do! He hoped to have a good sermon. It crossed his mind about talking on temperance, but he did not see just what that would have to do concerning the new buildings. He also remembered what Nadine had said about Rocky's drinking problem, and he agreed that anything that he could do, or say would change on jot or tittles, so finally leaving that in God's hands, he kind of came up blank, as to know what to talk about in his sermon.

The appointed day was narrowing down! He went to his private place near the river. There he thought, but mostly prayed for the right words to say. It seemed to him that this was the first time that he had had such a time making up something proper to say in his sermon. Dayton had came to the house, and announced that he had talked to his father on the phone, and the party, or so called celebration was shaping up, and it would be on the following week-end. So Jamie knew that he had to get with his sermon! As Jamie anticipated the coming event, he wondered again, just what happened to the quiet simple life that he had found for himself, and his family? It seemed that his brother Frankie had opened up Pandora's Box, and let out so much confusion! So much had happened since they came, and as much as Jamie rebuked against all this to himself, the bigger the situation got!

The day before the dedication, and the big celebration, there were all kinds of people showing up! There were the cooks, and catcaterscatersc, and musicians. The children helped really hard to set up big tents, and tables, and chairs. Jamie hoped that there would not blow up another storm like the one they had when Buddy got hurt. There sure would not be room for all those people in the cave shelter! As things started to take shape, Jamie realized that this was going to happen, and there was no way to stop it now, so he tried to have very little to do with it all! Rocky had it so planned out that there was not much for Jamie to do anyways! He just stood back, and marveled. Shaking his head to himself! He spent a lot of his time, by himself just working on his sermon, and praying for guidance as to what he should say.

The day of the big celebration finally arrived! All around the grounds there was tents, campers, and motor homes parked. It looked to Jamie just like a big camp meeting! He sort of accepted it as so. The new church was crowed, and when Jamie walked up to the pulpit, and looked out across the crowd, he saw so many faces that he knew! He did not realize that all his family from back home in Kentucky would be there! But knowing Rocky as he did, it would have been just like Rocky to have carted them all in by himself! He could not help but loving his friend! Jamie's sister Diane and her husband Steve was there. Rocky, and Bonnie, with all thirteen of their children. There was Frankie, Lorraine, and Lorramie. They were all there to greet and support him. He felt pretty nervous, but happy.

Dana sang her mother's song, 'He keeps me singing,' while Timmy played his guitar. Silence fell over the crowd, as she gave it her best performance. As Jamie listened to her song, he remembered his recent trip back to Kentucky, and Merle. He thought again on how much Dana looked like her mother, then a little sadness came over him, and tears filled his eyes, and he could not hardly see the faces in the pews, when he looked out upon them. They were all blurry to him!

After Dana and Timmy finished their special music, they took their seats in the audience. There was amens, and clapping. Then the church grew quiet, as Jamie stood up, and walked over to the pulpit. After he thanked Dana and Timmy for the sweet special music, he then prepared to give his sermon.

"JAMIE'S SERMON"
CHAPTER 25

"Family, and friends, and all those who came to worship in our new church building today. I want to welcome you all! It seems good to look out to so many faces! Better yet, so many familiar faces! I hope that your stay here in our little village will be a good remembrable one for you. It is just so great to have you all here, and I thank you all for coming!" He paused a minute, then continued;

"Early one morning, a while back, a bunch of men, oh, about four, or five, all dressed in disguise costumes, came to my home. They stood out in the yard, and called out, 'hey preacher, your church is burning!' Now that alone would have been hard enough to take, but being dressed in such strange costumes, made me realize that they did not want to be recognized, and also because of that, they had some mischief in their minds. I knew that these men meant to do me and my family some kind of harm! I do not even want to imagine just what they did have on their minds when they sat our church on fire! But they had hopes that I would rush off to the burning church, and leave my family unattended to. They wanted me to leave, so that they could take away my precious fair haired daughter, and have their way with her! They gave me a choice, like the devil himself would, and that was, either leave my family, and go help put the church fire out, which my first impressions was to do so! Or to let the church burn, and stay with my family, and deal with these men the best I could, either way, they thought that they could do as they

173

desired with my family, and hurt me that way! But the Lord told me to stay put! So I did the only thing that I could do, and that was to put the whole situation into God's hands. Well I choose to stay with my family, and let our church burn to the ground." Being all choked up, Jamie had to pause again. Then he spoke again.

"At one point, I felt I would not be able to stop those men, or the fire, except I knew that God has promised to always be with me, especially in the time of trouble! He was my helper, and he would provide me a way out. And God in His mercy for seen this thing, a long, long time ago! I mean, a few years back, maybe five or six years ago, our heavenly Father impressed a faithful earthly father, to teach his children right! This father, who was also bringing up my children too, took the time to teach them self-defense! He taught the Karate, or Marshall Arts, two of the same! And so, because this father was faithful in spending time and teaching the children, my son Timmy used what he had learned, by this faithful father, bravely, and may I add, manly, drove those evil men away!

"Now was this chance? Or was it being faithful to the pole, in what we ought to be doing? I thank God for faithful parents, especially this one, who not only did his job of teaching his child, but did my job too, by teaching my children right. I was not there, and he filled in for me! I must say, he did a great job! I now thank you my little brother! Also I thank God for all obedient children! They make me proud, and God will use them someday for His special work! Timmy looked at his uncle Frankie, and gave him a big smile.

"Also before this, God knew just what was going to happen that day! He also, impressed that same father to tell a friend about our need here at the mission. So allowing the Holy Spirit to lead, God put into motion, the building of a new church, before we actually needed one! He also added a bonus! A new school! Now all these young folks can be taught to read, and write, and who knows maybe the Marshall arts of protection! They will be taught to be strong, and followers of Him, our great Father! God's timing is always right on time! The very day that those men burnt our church down, a young man, who was also taught by faithful parents, came looking for me. He found me at the burning site. While I was at my lowest weak point, my best friend's son, so typical of his father, he gave me hope again! He told me that some funds were waiting for us! He said it was enough funds, already laid aside," He paused a minute, then he said;

"You heard me right! I said, 'already' laid aside, for what ever this mission needed! Now is that a good Father? Is that a good Friend! Yes, we have our earthly friends which may allow God to use them, but there is nothing, or nobody who is as great of a friend as our heavenly Father, who works through these earthly vessels!" Jamie paused, then there was some silence, then he went on.

"There was no doubt that we would have built the new church some day, regardless of the fire, but God had a time! He put the things in motion, so that it would happen in His right time! This proves to me, once again, that God is the Supreme King of Kings!

Dare show me another king as great as He is! He is the all-powerful, and all knowing sovereign God! What more can I say? What ever He promises or what ever He wishes for us, He is able to perform it for us! When He commands it, He also knows that it can be done! He also takes the responsibility! He uses many links in the chains of His purposes, but we some times fail to see, for we lack the faith to make it evident. We may want to take credit, maybe just a little bit, to make us feel important, but we could not do one littlest thing without God helping us to do it or without God even prompting us to do it! He uses His own time, and plans, and they are not always our times, and plans! Little by little, like putting a puzzle together, He works them out! We are all pieces of His great puzzle, and when one piece is missing, and then the puzzle is incomplete! We must not be impatient, and we must remember that God is not like us, for He does not lie! He does not have to repent! He does not have a deadline! He is not pushed, rushed, or impatient! He never needs to come up with a reason to, for what He says, He will do it! God knows, and attends to His own business. He keeps His Word! He is the Word! When we keep these thoughts in our minds, and our hearts, about God, then we can relax, and our worries and doubts disappear like the snow in the spring time!" Once again, Jamie paused; and there was silence, then he spoke again;

"This church project was not our project, it was God's project! For He ordained it, and because of this fact, it was not forsaken, because of lack of time, or funds, or interest of life. I profess to be a worker for God, and I know that the Lord will perfect that which concerned me!

The smallest of animals on this earth, are just as safe as the biggest ones, because it has nothing to do with the bigness of things. It is not the importance that we feel we are, it has to do with being under the shadow of God Almighty! Safely tucked under His wing! When HE confirms us, we will be safe, and secure forever! What kind of a God would He be, if He did not do this for us?" Once again he paused for a few second, and then he went on.

"Sometimes, it appears that a Christian is forgotten, or over looked by God, and because of this, the heathens think that a Christian is a fool to serve the Lord, who has not prospered them materially, or even physically, for they are comparing the Christian to the worldly standards, which is not the way of God. With God, the spirit, or the soul comes first. So if we die in the flesh, we still remain alive in the spirit! But I must say here, we who are Christians, have a promise that the unchristian, or heathens do not have, and can not attain while remaining in the unchristian way, and that is this, being confident of this very thing, which is this…that God has begun a good work in you the Christian, and He will perform it until the day of Jesus Christ's return. For He never leaves you, or forsakes you, like the devil will try to make you believe. If you go by your feelings, you may think, or feel that God has forsaken you, but He has not! Remember our feelings, and thinking is not anywhere like His! Do not try to compare them at all! If you do, you will be let down by your own thoughts and feelings! Stay away from them, do not even go there!" Jamie paused again then went on.

"While building the church, one of the young men who were working, fell off the scaffold, and was hurt badly. He needed an operation, and he needed blood! Well today that young man and I are now blood brothers, because both of us had a rare type blood. My blood type matched his, and so I had the opportunity to give my blood to him to help save his life. I was glad I could be in the right place at the right time! I was glad that I could help save his life! I tell this story, not because I want to take any credit, but to illustrate to you, that Jesus donated His blood to save you, and me from death eternal! If this young man had died, he still would have had a chance for heaven, with or without my blood, but if we die without the blood of Christ, we will die forever, eternal! Jesus was glad, and proud that He could do it for us too! He is our ever lasting brother! Our Saviour! Yes, Jesus, who can save our souls, can also save us from our evil sinful ways! Trust me! I know! Our everyday, going about being our selves, we perform habits that we get so use to doing, or we have no will power to get out of them, so we just do not stop and realize that they will eventually kill us! Not only our bodies, but our souls! Which by the way is very permanent? Permanent enough to keep us out of heaven! The worst thing about these bad habits is, that we perform them without even thinking of the bad results, or the dangers we not only put our selves into but we put others in danger too! Maybe even our loved ones! You know if we take the time to see, and realize that we have these bad habits, we can come boldly to the throne of Grace, and confess them, stating to our heavenly Father that we do not want to do them anymore, He is faithful, and just to forgive us our sins, and cleans us from all unrighteousness. We even get a starter kit with this package. He will give us the grace to never want to think about that habit again!" Jamie paused again then went on;

"Like the new church building that has nothing yet to defile it, so with Jesus' help, we can be undefiled before God. Just think God treated His Son Jesus Christ on the cross, as he should have treated us, and He treats us as if we where Jesus Christ! Because we are all of one body! Imagine! The Spirit of Christ is the Holy Spirit of God Himself, and only He can give us that Christ like nature." Once again he paused, and then continued;

"Today is a special day, for today we want to dedicate our new church, and school building to God. We want His blessings upon it! We want His Spirit to dwell there within its walls, and we want also for Him to impart His Spirit to all those who came to seek Him there. We want to find His peace, and comfort there! We cried unto the Lord in our troubles, and He heard us before we even asked, and saved us out of our distress. He brought us out of the darkness, and into the light of His love. He brought us out from under the shadow of death! Oh that we would praise the Lord for His goodness, and for His wonderful works to the children of men. He allows trouble to beset us, so that we may come to Him. He gives us the right, now will you not come to Him now with repentance! Let us bow our heads in prayer." Jamie said, and all bowed their heads.

"Our precious Father in heaven, we want to thank you so much for sending us this new church, and church school building. We want Your Spirit to dwell here amonst us. We ask that your blessings remain upon these buildings, and please send Your saving power to those who worked faithfully with you to make this all possible. You impressed them to help, and they heeded, and obeyed Your voice. I ask that You continue to bless them, and impress them all in the way You see fit. I ask this prayer in Jesus' name who holds all power, let Thy will be done on earth, as it is in heaven. AMEN>

ABOUT THE AUTHOR

Dorothy LaRock Skinner was born in upstate New York. She was the youngest of a family of ten. She went to school in Constableville, N.Y. It was during her high school years that she decided that she wanted to be a writer. She was always writing stories, and poems. It was while she was still in high school that she wrote the story of "JAMIE".

She graduated there in 1958. She then went on to Atlantic Union College, in South Lancaster, Mass, where she studied to become an elementary teacher.

On her return home, she met, a farmer named Luther Skinner. They was married in October of 1960, and then lived on the Skinner Farm, located in Camden, N.Y.

In the fall of 1961, they had their first child, which she named him Jamie, after the man in her story.

She remained a free lance writer, and sold her writings to different magazines.

Her second child was born in 1965, and she named her Rebecca.

In 1972, she took a course in writing for children. She received her diploma from "The Institute of Children's Literature." While still writing short stories for children, she had her third child, Jeremy, which was born in 1975.

In 1977, her and her husband bought a larger farm, located on the Howd Road, still in Camden, N>Y> Now that they was a full time farmer, it took up a lot of her time, yet she still found the time to write.

She has written several different stories, along with her life story, which she is still working on. Her plans are that she someday will have her life story published.

Since the story of "JAMIE" was her first born story ever, it has been her life long dream to see it published. She hopes that you will soon be reading her story.

Printed in the United States
19266LVS00007B/76-93

9 781418 423469